SOLDIERS THREE

A. H. WHEELER & Cº'S
INDIAN RAILWAY LIBRARY

Nº 1.   BY

Rudyard Kipling

ONE RUPEE.

LAHORE

The R. S. Surtees Society is most grateful to Lady Juliet Townsend (The Old Hall Bookshop, Market Place, Brackley) and to David Robertshaw (The Warminster Bookshop, 6 East Street, Warminster) for lending the books from which the covers and texts of the Kipling titles in the Indian Railway Library series have been – or are about to be – copied; we are also very grateful to John Saumarez Smith (G. Heywood Hill, 10 Curzon Street, London, W.1.) for most opportunely suggesting where we might find what we were looking for.

We were delighted when Philip Mason agreed to write Forewords for *Soldiers Three* and *The Story of the Gadsbys* and still more pleased when he agreed, with apparent alacrity, to provide Forewords for *In Black and White* and *Under the Deodars,* which we intend shall be avialable by April, 1987.

Our publication of *Soldiers Three* and *The Story of the Gadsbys* is by permission of Macmillan London Limited.

───────────

In our leaflet of May 1986 we advertised our books as facsimiles of the first editions published in the Indian Railway Library series in 1888, save for the addition, in the case of *Soldiers Three,* of four illustrations by A. S. Hartrick. After the issue of the leaflet we decided on the further additions to *Soldiers Three* of 'Danny Deever' and 'The 'Eathen'. It may be that some pre-publication subscribers subscribed on the assumption that we would do exactly what we said we would do and that to these we now owe such explanation as is available.

Professor Sir Angus Wilson has written that the exploits of the three soldiers are best read alongside *Barrack Room Ballads.*

An inattentive reader of 'In the Matter of a Private' might be left with the impression that the author made the fate of Private Simmons too light a matter. 'Danny Deever', No. 1 of *Barrack Room Ballads* and first published in the *Scots Observer* in February 1890 (which separates it by months, rather than years, from 'In the Matter of a Private', first published in April 1888), should correct any such impression.

Similarly some readers might just possibly suppose that 'With the Main Guard' was a callous indulgence of the public's taste for military vainglory, with a remarkable example of a late

Victorian's complacent idea of the devotion of the lower orders (at any rate, when in uniform) to the officer and gentlemanly class thrown in for good measure. Inclusion of 'The 'Eathen' may make it clear that 'With the Main Guard' is a story about comradeship – how Mulvaney, with some help from Ortheris, generously used his histrionic gift to rescue Learoyd from Giant Despair, to such effect that at the end of the story Learoyd is himself helping a comrade, or at any rate helping to help his child. In another story Learoyd and Ortheris perform a similar service for Mulvaney and, they having shifted Mulvaney away from tragedy to the ordinarily melancholy, the author unobstrusively moves all three on to cheerfulness by providing bottled beer – for free. Golly, how the Liberals must have hated him!

'The 'Eathen' first appeared in McClure's Magazine in 1896. Professor Sir Charles Carrington has said that the lines

'So, like a man in irons which isn't glad to go,

They moves 'em off by companies uncommon stiff an' slow.'
are the most compelling proof of Kipling's imaginative powers. He says that he would not have believed it possible for a man, who had never himself seen infantry move when required to close with the enemy, to pen such an exact description. So for those of us who have not been present on such occasions (Carrington has) the verses are informative.

We were over confident when we said in the leaflet that the covers were designed by Rudyard's father, Lockwood Kipling. All that is known with certainty (we now think) is that the covers were designed at the Mayo School of Art, Lahore, of which Lockwood was the Director.

We would have liked to have exercised our literary intuition by telling readers that the dog momentarily stationary behind Jock Learoyd's heels, on the cover of *Soldiers Three,* is a portrait of Rudyard's fox-terrier Vic (or Vixen as she is called when she appears in Literature). But a comtemporary of Rudyard, quoted by Angus Wilson, wrote that Vic was white "like a nice clean sucking pig" whereas the dog in the picture has extensive black markings. Rip, whom Mrs. DeSussa coveted, is a possibility.

Lastly, following our principle of telling the truth unless it is intolerably inconvenient, anyone who consults James McG.

Stewart's Bibliographical Catalogue of Kipling (published by Dalhousie University, Canada) will note some further divergences from the first Indian editions which we have not mentioned here.

James McG. Stewart is the chap. Borrowing a first Indian edition would be, at best, difficult and troublesome; and honest acquisition very expensive.

R.S.S.S.
Rockfield House,
Nunney, Nr. Frome,
Somerset. Aug. 1986

THE R. S. SURTEES SOCIETY

First published in this edition in 1986 by
The R. S. Surtees Society

Rockfield House
Nunney
Nr. Frome, Somerset

© This Edition and Compilation
The R. S. Surtees Society, 1986
ISBN 0 948560 03 7

Produced in Great Britain
by MARCH PRESS,
Adderwell Road, Frome, Somerset.

FOREWORD

To many people the name of Kipling will suggest the certainty of his political convictions, which were of a very conservative kind. But to his seniors when he first arrived in India – straight from school and just before he was seventeen – he often seemed not merely cocky but subversive. He was a 'cub reporter' for the *Civil and Military Gazette* in Lahore and though he duly carried out the routine duties of the newspaper he was constantly looking for chances to express himself by imaginative writing. When a new editor gave him a much freer hand, he displayed an astonishing variety of moods and subjects, some of which disturbed and even shocked his readers.

Forty of these first imaginative sketches were published as *Plain Tales from the Hills.* Among them are four about private soldiers in a battalion of British infantry, Mulvaney, Learoyd and Otheris. *Plain Tales* was published in 1888, when Kipling was 22; the same year saw the publication of six further collections of similar, but rather longer, stories, in Wheeler's *Indian Railway Library.* One of these volumes was *Soldiers Three,* paper backed and priced at One Rupee – about the fifteenth part of a pound sterling. It contained seven stories, all but one about the already famous three. There were to be three more in *Life's Handicap,* three in *Many Inventions* and one in *Actions and Reactions.*

Soldiers Three was published again in England in 1890 and it was these stories that first made Kipling famous. They must have come as a shock to many, both in England and in India. Polite literature ignored the serving soldier and drawing-rooms did not mention him. Now here he was, pugnacious, brutal, fond of his beer, but a man, who loved and hated, felt remorse and pity. Above all, he has a strong sense of personal self-respect and of his honour as a soldier. It was disturbing to be told that this vital creature was a living human part of Queen Victoria's respectable England.

In those early years, the young Kipling was far from sure of himself; he was searching for a voice of his own and themes of his own. Rather more than half the stories in *Plain Tales* are about English people in India, officers and their wives, members of the club; in the rest he is exploring new worlds and one of these is the world of the private soldier. In 1890, in a London music-hall, he had a moment of vision and wrote to his *confidante* Mrs. Hill that 'the people of London require a poet of the Music Halls'. He began to feel that it was his task in life to convey 'in a popular form' 'basic and basaltic' truths about human nature. This was what started him on *Barrack Room Ballads* and he said once that for a time whenever the idea occurred to him of a *Soldiers Three* story, he gave it precedence over everything else.

The 'popular form' disgusted some intellectuals. So did the brutality and pugnacity which were part of the 'basaltic truth'. The *Soldiers Three* stories are sometimes farcical and some-times Mulvaney is a secret manipulator behind the scenes, as Stalky was to become. But basically they are about serious things. André Maurois said of Kipling that he had 'a permanent natural contact with the oldest and deepest layers of human con-sciousness'. These stories are shot through with remorse for lost innocence, for lost opportunities, for lost love. It was love gone wrong that had led Learoyd to enlist and not only Learoyd. Death is never far away, by cholera or typhoid, by an enemy's bullet, by murder or suicide.

The men slept near their rifles; they had quick access to live ammunition. They had many long hours with nothing to do but brood on the emptiness of their lives and the wrongs which Fate – or a sergeant or a comrade – had put upon them. 'Barrack-room shootings' were a regular feature of the hot weather in India; Kipling had had to report them for his paper. 'They're hanging Danny Deever in the morning' – that searing poem was based on something Kipling had seen happen and some of these stories are about why it happened. Two of these seven – *In the Matter of a Private* and *Black Jack* are directly concerned with murder or attempted murder and another with despair that might lead to suicide. At one time or another, each of the three friends is near to suicide or desertion, which is nearly as bad.

To most of us today, the convention as regards dialect which Kipling followed is an obstacle. A hundred years later a skilful writer will suggest an Irish brogue by the turn of the sentence, the choice of words, only an occasional mis-spelling. But Kipling tries to reproduce phonetically what he has heard. 'Fwhy is ut, Sorr?' Mulvaney says – and worse still, 'a shuparflous an' impart'nint observashin'. And it is Mulvaney who tells most of the stories. It is tiring to the reader; it demands a slight effort of translation. But it is worth making the effort, and once the swing of the story grips you, the dialect is forgotten. Mulvaney is a tragic figure masquerading as comic, and three of the soldier stories – *The Courting of Dinah Shadd, On Greenhow Hill,* and *Love o' Women* – have been reckoned by some judges among the best Kipling wrote. Those three came after the seven included in this volume, *Love o' Women,* the last, having been published in 1893, when Kipling was 27; they are longer than these seven, a shade more mature, more carefully constructed, more passionatly felt. But *Black Jack* comes near them.

There is no evidence that Kipling had a special friendship with three soldiers who resembled the famous three. They are composite figures based on a number of actual soldiers he had met, brought alive by his imagination.

This volume contains the seven first printed together in India as *Soldiers Three* and later republished in England in a form as nearly as possible that of the first edition, which made Kipling's name.

Hither Daggons,   PHILIP MASON
Cripplestyle,   May 1986
Alderholt,
Nr. Fordingbridge,
Hampshire.

OPINIONS OF THE PRESS.

The *Spectator* says :—As a wholesome corrective to what may be called the oleographic style of depicting military life now so much in vogue, Mr. Kipling's brilliant sketches of the barrack-room, realistic in the best sense of the word, deserve a hearty welcome. Here be no inanities of the officers' mess, no apotheosis of the gilded and tawny-moustachioed dragoon, no languid and lisping lancer, no child-sweet-hearts—none, in fact, of the sentimental paraphernalia familiar to readers of modern military fiction. Here, instead, we have Tommy Atkins as the central figure, and not Tommy Atkins on parade, but in those moods when the natural man finds freest expression—amorous, pugnacious, and thievish—a somewhat earthy personage on the whole, but with occasional gleams of chivalry and devotion lighting up his clouded humanity. Too many so-called realists seem to aim at repre-senting man as continuously animal without any intervals in which his higher nature emerges at all. But Mr. Kipling happily does not belong to this school. The actualities of barrack-room life are not extenuated, but the tone of the whole is sound and manly. The author does not gloss over the animal tendencies of the British private, but he shows how in the grossest natures sparks of nobility may lie hid.

The perusal of these stories cannot fail to inspire the reader with the desire to make further acquaintance with the other writings of the author. They are brimful of humanity and a drollery that never degenerates into burlesque. In many places a note of genuine pathos is heard. Mr. Kipling is so gifted and versatile that one would gladly see him at work on a larger canvas. But to be so brilliant a teller of short stories is in itself no small distinction.

The *Saturday Review* says :—The *Story of the Gadsbys* is well con-structed and humorous in a high degree, and exhibits the author's thorough acquaintance with Anglo-Indian life. Most readers who like sequels will, no doubt, prefer his own story, where they will meet again the Irishman, Mulvaney, and his brother musketeers.

The *Admiralty and Horse Guards Gazette* says :—We can only regret that these two books are not published in England. Of the two, *Soldiers Three* is, we think, the best. It shows a very thorough know-ledge of the character of the British soldier and his Indian surround-ings, while *The Story of the Gadsbys*, though not quite such agreeable reading, will still be read with amusement by all who know anything of Indian life. No one can read the various stories in *Soldiers Three* without being immensely tickled with the vast amount of real wit contained in the dialogue.

SOLDIERS THREE:

A COLLECTION OF STORIES

SETTING FORTH CERTAIN PASSAGES IN THE LIVES AND ADVEN-
TURES OF PRIVATES TERENCE MULVANEY, STANLEY
ORTHERIS, AND JOHN LEAROYD.

BY

RUDYARD KIPLING.

" We be Soldiers Three——
Pardonnez moi, je vous en prie."

ALLAHABAD:
PRINTED AT THE "PIONEER" PRESS.

1888

To

THAT VERY STRONG MAN,

T. ATKINS,

PRIVATE OF THE LINE,

THIS BOOK IS DEDICATED

IN ALL ADMIRATION AND GOODFELLOWSHIP.

PREFACE.

THIS small book contains, for the most part, the further adventures of my esteemed friends and sometime allies, Privates Mulvaney, Ortheris, and Learoyd, who have already been introduced to the public. Those anxious to know how the three most cruelly maltreated a Member of Parliament; how Ortheris went mad for a space; how Mulvaney and some friends took the town of Lungtungpen; and how little Jhansi McKenna helped the regiment when it was smitten with cholera, must refer to a book called *Plain Tales from the Hills.* I would have reprinted the four stories in this place, but Dinah Shadd says that "tearin' the tripes out av a book wid a pictur' on the back, all to make Terence proud past reasonin'," is wasteful, and Mulvaney himself says that he prefers to have his fame "dishpersed most notoriously in sev'ril volumes". I can only hope that his desire will be gratified.

RUDYARD KIPLING.

CONTENTS.

~~~~~~~~~

THE GOD FROM THE MACHINE.

Hit a man an' help a woman, an' ye can't be far wrong anyways.—
Maxims of Private Mulvaney.

THE Inexpressibles gave a ball. They borrowed a seven-pounder from the Gunners, and wreathed it with laurels, and made the dancing-floor plateglass, and provided a supper the like of which had never been eaten before, and set two sentries at the door of the room to hold the trays of programme-cards. My friend Private Mulvaney was one of the sentries, because he was the tallest man in the regiment. When the dance was fairly started the sentries were released, and Private Mulvaney fled to curry favour with the Mess Sergeant in charge of the supper. Whether the Mess Sergeant gave or Mulvaney took, I cannot say. All that I am certain of is that, at supper-time, I found Mulvaney with Private Ortheris, two-thirds of a ham, a loaf of bread, half a pâté-de-foie-gras and two magnums of champagne, sitting on the roof of my carriage. As I came up I heard him saying :—

"Praise be a danst doesn't come as often as Ord'ly-room, or, by this an' that, Orth'ris, me son, I wud be the dishgrace av the rig'mint instid av the brightest jool in uts crown ".

"*Hand* the Colonel's pet noosince," said Ortheris, who was a Londoner. "But wot makes you curse your rations ? This 'ere fizzy stuff's good enough."

"Stuff, ye oncivilised pagin ! 'Tis champagne we're dhrinkin' now. 'Tisn't that I am set agin. 'Tis this quare stuff wid the little bits av black leather in it. I misdoubt I will be distressin'ly sick wid it in the mornin'. Fwhat is ut?"

"Goose liver," I said, climbing on the top of the carriage,

for I knew that it was better to sit out with Mulvaney than to dance many dances.

"Goose liver is ut?" said Mulvaney. "Faith, I'm thinkin' thim that makes it wud do betther to cut up the Colonel. He carries a power av liver undher his right arrum whin the days are warm an' the nights chill. He wud give thim tons an' tons av liver. 'Tis he sez so. 'I'm all liver to-day,' sez he; an' wid that he ordhers me ten days C. B. for as moild a dhrink as iver a good sodger tuk betune his teeth."

"That was when 'e wanted for to wash 'isself in the Fort Ditch," Ortheris explained. "'Said there was too much beer in the Barrack water-butts for a God-fearing man. You was lucky in gettin' orf with wot you did, Mulvaney."

"You say so? Now I'm pershuaded I was cruel hard trated—seein' fwhat I've done for the likes av him in the days whin my eyes were wider opin than they are now. Man alive, for the Colonel to whip *me* on the peg in that way! Me that have saved the repitation av a ten times better man than him! 'Twas ne-farious, an' that manes a power av evil!"

"Never mind the nefariousness!" I said. "Whose reputation did you save?"

"More's the pity, 'twasn't my own, but I tuk more trouble wid ut than av ut was. 'Twas just my way, messin' wid fwhat was no business av mine. Hear now!" He settled himself at ease on the top of the carriage. "I'll tell you all about ut. Av coorse I will name no names, for there's wan that's an orf'cer's lady now, that was in ut, and no more will I name places, for a man is thracked by a place."

"Eyah!" said Ortheris, lazily, "but this is a mixed story wot's comin'."

"Wanst upon a time, as the childer-books say, I was a recruity."

"Was you though?" said Ortheris; "now that's extry-ordinary!"

"Orth'ris," said Mulvaney, "av you opin thim lips av yours again, I will, savin' your presince, Sorr, take you by the slack av your trousers an' heave you."

"I'm mum," said Ortheris. "Wot 'appened when you was a recruity?"

"I was a betther recruity than you iver was or will be, but that's neither here nor there. Thin I became a man, an' the divil of a man I was fifteen years ago. They called me Buck Mulvaney in thim days, an', begad, I tuk a woman's eye. I did that! Ortheris, ye scrub, fwhat are ye sniggerin' at? Do you misdoubt me?"

"Devil a doubt!" said Ortheris; "but I've 'eard summat like that before!"

Mulvaney dismissed the impertinence with a lofty wave of his hand and continued:—

"An' the orf'cers av the rig'mint I was in in thim days *was* orf'cers—gran' men, wid a manner on 'em, an' a way wid 'em such as is not made these days—all but wan—wan o' the Capt'ns. A bad dhrill, a wake voice, an' a limp leg—thim three things are the signs av a bad man. You bear that in your hid, Orth'ris, me son.

"An' the Colonel av the rig'mint had a daughter—wan av thim lamblike, bleatin', pick-me-up-an'-carry-me-or-I'll-die gurls such as was made for the natural prey av men like the Capt'n who was iverlastin' payin' coort to her, though the Colonel he said time an' over: 'Kape out av the brute's way, my dear'. But he niver had the heart for to send her away from the throuble, bein' as he was a widower, an' she their wan child."

"Stop a minute, Mulvaney," said I; "how in the world did you come to know these things?"

"How did I come?" said Mulvaney, with a scornful grunt; "bekaze I'm turned durin' the Quane's pleasure to a lump av wood, lookin' out straight forninst me, wid a—a—candelabbrum in my hand, for you to pick your cards out av, must I not see nor feel? Av coorse I du! Up my back, an'

in my boots, an' in the short hair av the neck—that's where
I kape my eyes whin I'm on duty an' the reg'lar wans are
fixed.   Know! Take my word for it, Sorr, ivrything an' a
great dale more is known in a rig'mint; or fwhat wud be the
use av a Mess Sargint, or a Sargint's wife doin' wet-nurse to
the Major's baby? To reshume. He was a bad dhrill was
this Capt'n—a rotten bad dhrill—an' whin first I ran me eye
over him, I sez to myself : 'My Militia bantam!' I sez, 'my
cock av a Gosport dunghill'—'twas from Portsmouth he came
to us—'there's combs to be cut,' sez I, 'an' by the grace av
God, 'tis Terence Mulvaney will cut thim'.

" So he wint menowderin', and minanderin, an' blandan-
dhering roun' an' about the Colonel's daughter, an' she, poor
innocint, lookin' at him like a Comm'ssariat bullock looks at
the Comp'ny cook. He'd a dhirty little scrub av a black
moustache, an' he twisted an' turned ivry wurrd he used as
av he found ut too sweet for to spit out. Eyah! He was a
tricky man an' a liar by natur'. Some are born so. He was
wan. I knew he was over his belt in money borrowed from
natives ; besides a lot av other mathers which, in regard
for your presince, Sorr, I will oblitherate. A little av fwhat
I knew, the Colonel knew, for he wud have none av him,
an' that, I'm thinkin', by fwhat happened aftherwards, the
Capt'n knew.

" Wan day, bein' mortial idle, or they wud never ha'
thried ut, the rig'mint gave amshure theatricals—orf'cers an'
orf'cers' ladies. You've seen the likes time an' agin, Sorr, an'
poor fun 'tis for them that sit in the back row an' stamp wid
their boots for the honour av the rig'mint. I was told off for
to shif' the scenes, haulin' up this an' draggin' down that.
Light work ut was, wid lashins av beer and the gurl that
dhressed the orf'cers' ladies . . . but she died in Aggra twelve
years gone, an' my tongue's gettin' the betther av me. They
was actin' a play thing called *Sweethearts*, which you may ha'
heard av, an' the Colonel's daughter she was a lady's maid.
The Capt'n was a boy called Broom—Spread Broom was his

name in the play. Thin I saw—ut come out in the actin'
—fwhat I niver saw before, an' that was that he was no
gentleman. They was too much together, thim two, a-
whishperin' behind the scenes I shifted, an' some av what
they said I heard; for I was death—blue death an' ivy—on
the comb-cuttin'. He was iverlastin'ly oppressing her to fall
in wid some sneakin' schame av his, an' she was thryin' to
stand out against him, but not as though she was set in her
will. I wonder now in thim days that my ears did not grow
a yard on me head wid list'nin'. But I looked straight
forninst me, an' hauled up this an' dragged down that, such
as was my duty, an' the orf'cers' ladies sez one to another,
thinkin' I was out av listen-reach: 'Fwhat an obligin' young
man is this Corp'ril Mulvaney!' I was a Corp'ril then. I
was rejuced afthwards, but, no matther, I was a Corp'ril
wanst.

"Well, this *Sweethearts'* business wint on like most
amshure theatricals, an' barrin' fwhat I suspicioned, 'twasn't
till the dhress-rehearsal that I saw for certain that thim two
—he the blackguard, an' she no wiser than she should ha'
been—had put up an evasion."

"A what?" said I.

"E-vasion! Fwhat you lorruds an' ladies call an elope-
mint. E-vasion I calls it, bekaze, exceptin' whin 'tis right
an' natural an' proper, 'tis wrong an' dhirty to steal a man's
wan child not knowin' her own mind. There was a Sargint
in the Comm'ssariat who set my face upon e-vasions. I'll
tell you about that ——"

"Stick to the bloomin' Captains, Mulvaney," said Ortheris;
"Comm'ssariat Sargints is low."

Mulvaney accepted the emendation and went on:—

"Now I knew that the Colonel was no fool, any more
than me, for I was hild the smartest man in the rig'mint, an'
the Colonel was the best orf'cer commandin' in Asia; so fwhat
he said an' I said was a mortial truth. We knew that the
Capt'n was bad, but, for reasons which I have already

oblitherated, I knew more than me Colonel.   I wud ha'
rolled out his face wid the butt av my gun before permittin'
av him to steal the gurl.   Saints knew av he wud ha' married
her, and av he didn't she wud be in great tormint, an' the
divil av what you, Sorr, call a 'scandal'.   But I niver sthruck,
niver raised me hand on my shuperior orf'cer; an' that was a
merricle now I come to considher it."

   "Mulvaney, the dawn's risin'," said Ortheris, "an' we're
no nearer 'ome than we was at the beginnin'.   Lend me your
pouch.   Mine's all dust."

   Mulvaney pitched his pouch across, and filled his pipe
afresh.

   "So the dhress-rehearsal came to an end, an', bekaze I
was curious, I stayed behind whin the scene-shiftin' was
ended, an' I shud ha' been in barricks, lyin' as flat as a toad
under a painted cottage thing.   They was talkin' in whispers,
an' she was shiverin' an' gaspin' like a fresh-hukked fish.
'Are you sure you've got the hang av the manewvers?' sez
he, or wurrds to that effec', as the coort martial sez.   'Sure
as death,' sez she, 'but I misdoubt 'tis cruel hard on my
father.'   'Damn your father,' sez he, or any ways 'twas fwhat
he thought, 'the arrangement is as clear as mud.   Jungi will
drive the carr'ige afther all's over, an' you come to the station,
cool an' aisy, in time for the two o'clock thrain, where I'll
be wid your kit.'   'Faith,' thinks I to myself, 'thin there's a
ayah in the business tu!'

   "A powerful bad thing is a ayah.   Don't you niver have
any thruck wid wan.   Thin he began sootherin' her, an' all
the orf'cers an' orf'cers' ladies left, an' they put out the lights.
To explain the theory av the flight, as they say at Muskthry,
you must understand that afther this *Sweethearts'* nonsinse
was ended, there was another little bit av a play called *Couples*
—some kind av couple or another.   The gurl was actin' in this,
but not the man.   I suspicioned he'd go to the station wid the
gurl's kit at the end av the first piece.   'Twas the kit that
flusthered me for I knew for a Capt'n to go trapesing about

the impire wid the lord knew what av a *truso* on his arrum was nefarious, an' wud be worse than easin' the flag, so far as the talk aftherwards wint."

" 'Old on, Mulvaney. Wot's *truso?*" said Ortheris.

"You're an oncivilised man, me son. Whin a gurl's married, all her kit an' 'coutrements are *truso,* which manes weddin'-portion. An' 'tis the same whin she's runnin' away, even wid the biggest blackguard on the Arrmy List.

"So I made my plan av campaign. The Colonel's house was a good two miles away. 'Dennis,' sez I to my Colour-Sargint, ' av you love me lend me your kyart, for me heart is bruk an' me feet is sore wid trampin' to and from this foolish-ness at the Gaff. An' Dennis lent ut, wid a rampin', stampin' red stallion in the shafts. Whin they was all settled down to their *Sweethearts* for the first scene, which was a long wan, I slips outside and into the kyart. Mother av Hivin! but I made that horse walk, an' we came into the Colonel's compound as the divil wint through Athlone—in standin' leps. There was no one there excipt the servints, an' I wint round to the back an' found the girl's ayah.

" ' Ye black brazen Jezebel,' sez I, ' sellin' your masther's honour for five rupees—pack up all the Miss Sahib's kit an' look slippy! *Capt'n Sahib's* order,' sez I; ' going to the station we are,' I sez, an' wid that I laid my finger to my nose an' looked the schamin' sinner I was.

" ' *Bote acchy,*' sez she; so I knew she was in the business, an' I piled up all the sweet talk I'd iver learnt in the bazars on to this she-bullock, an' prayed av her to put all the quick she knew into the thing. While she packed, I stud outside an' sweated, for I was wanted for to shif' the second scene. I tell you, a young gurl's e-vasion manes as much baggage as a rig'mint on the line av march! 'Saints help Dennis's springs,' thinks I, as I bundled the stuff into the thrap, 'for I'll have no mercy!'

" ' I'm comin' too,' says the ayah.

" ' No, you don't,' sez I, ' later—*pechy!* You *baito* where

2

you are.   I'll *pechy* come an' bring you *sart*, along with me, you maraudin'—niver mind fwhat I called her.

"Thin I wint for the Gaff, an' by the special ordher av Providence, for I was doin' a good work you will ondersthand, Dennis's springs hild toight.   'Now, whin the Capt'n goes for that kit,' thinks I, 'he'll be throubled.'   At the end av *Sweethearts* off the Capt'n runs in his kyart to the Colonel's house, an' I sits down on the steps and laughs.   Wanst an' again I slipped in to see how the little piece was goin', an' whin ut was near endin' I stepped out all among the carriages an' sings out very softly, 'Jungi!'   Wid that a carr'ge began to move, an' I waved to the dhriver.   '*Hitherao!*' sez I, an' he *hitheraoed* till I judged he was at proper distance, an' thin I tuk him, fair an' square betune the eyes, all I knew for good or bad, an' he dhropped wid a guggle like the canteen beer-engine whin ut's runnin' low.   Thin I ran to the kyart an' tuk out all the kit an' piled it into the carr'ge, the sweat runnin' down my face in dhrops.   'Go home,' sez I, to the *sais ;* 'you'll find a man close here.   Very sick he is. Take him away, an' av you iver say wan wurrd about fwhat you've *dekkoed*, I'll *marrow* you till your own wife won't *sumjao* who you are!'   Thin I heard the stampin' av feet at the ind av the play, an' I ran in to let down the curtain. Whin they all came out the gurl thried to hide herself behind wan av the pillars, an' sez 'Jungi' in a voice that wudn't ha' scared a hare.   I run over to Jungi's carr'ge an' tuk up the lousy old horse-blanket on the box, wrapped my head an' the rest av me in ut, an' dhrove up to where she was.

"'Miss Sahib,' sez I; 'Going to the station ? *Captain Sahib's* order!' an' widout a sign she jumped in all among her own kit.

"I laid to an' dhruv like steam to the Colonel's house before the Colonel was there, an' she screamed an' I thought she was goin' off.   Out comes the ayah, saying all sorts av things about the Capt'n havin' come for the kit an' gone to the station.

"'Take out the luggage, you divil,' sez I, 'or I'll murther you !'

" The lights av the thraps people comin' from the Gaff was showin' acrost the parade ground, an', by this an' that, the way thim two women worked at the bundles an' thrunks was a caution ! I was dyin' to help, but, seein' I didn't want to be known, I sat wid the blanket roun' me an' coughed an' thanked the Saints there was no moon that night.

" Whin all was in the house again, I niver asked for *buk-shish* but dhruv tremenjus in the opp'site way from the other carr'ge an' put out my lights. Presintly, I saw a naygur man wallowin' in the road. I slipped down before I got to him, for I suspicioned Providence was wid me all through that night. 'Twas Jungi, his nose smashed in flat, all dumb sick as you please. Dennis's man must have tilted him out av the thrap. Whin he came to, ' Hutt ! ' sez I, but he began to howl.

" ' You black lump av dirt,' I sez, ' is this the way you dhrive your *gharri ?* That *tikka* has been *owin'* an' *fere-owin'* all over the bloomin' country this whole bloomin' night, an' you as *mut-walla* as Davey's sow. Get up, you hog ! ' sez I, louder, for I heard the wheels av a thrap in the dark ; ' get up an' light your lamps, or you'll be run into ! ' This was on the road to the Railway Station.

" ' Fwhat the divil's this ? ' sez the Capt'n's voice in the dhark, an' I could judge he was in a lather av rage.

" ' *Gharri* dhriver here, dhrunk, Sorr,' sez I ; ' I've found his *gharri* sthrayin' about cantonmints, an' now I've found *him.*'

" ' Oh ! ' sez the Capt'n ; ' fwhat's his name ? ' I stooped down an' pretended to listen.

" ' He sez his name's Jungi,' Sorr, sez I.

" ' Hould my harse,' sez the Capt'n to his man, an' wid that he gets down wid the whip an' lays into Jungi, just mad wid rage an' swearin' like the scutt he was.

" I thought, afther a while, he wud kill the man, so I sez :—' Stop, Sorr, or you'll murdher him ! ' That dhrew all his fire on me, an' he cursed me into Blazes, an' out again.

I stud to attenshin an' saluted :—'Sorr,' sez I, 'av ivry man in this wurruld had his rights, I'm thinkin' that more than wan wud be beaten to a shakin' jelly for this night's work— that never came off at all, Sorr, as you see ?' ' Now,' thinks I to myself, 'Terence Mulvaney, you've cut your own throat, for he'll sthrike, an' you'll knock him down for the good av his sowl an' your own iverlastin' dishgrace !'

"But the Capt'n never said a single wurrd. He choked where he stud, an' thin he went into his thrap widout sayin' good night, an' I wint back to barricks."

" And then ? " said Ortheris and I together.

"That was all," said Mulvaney; "niver another word did I hear av the whole thing. All I know was that there was no e-vasion, an' that was fwhat I wanted. Now, I put ut to you, Sorr, is ten days' C. B. a fit an' a proper tratement for a man who has behaved as me ? "

"Well, any'ow," said Ortheris, " 'tweren't this 'ere Colonel's daughter, an' you was blazin' copped when you tried to wash in the Fort Ditch."

"That," said Mulvaney, finishing the champagne, " is a shuparfluous an' impert'nint observation."

PRIVATE LEAROYD'S STORY.

" And he told a tale."—*Chronicles of Gautama Buddha.*

FAR from the haunts of Company Officers who insist upon kit-inspections, far from keen-nosed Sergeants who sniff the pipe stuffed into the bedding-roll, two miles from the tumult of the barracks, lies the Trap. It is an old dry well, shadowed by a twisted *pipal* tree and fenced with high grass. Here, in the years gone by, did Private Ortheris establish his depôt and menagerie for such possessions living and dead as could not safely be introduced to the barrack-room. Here were gathered Houdin pullets, and fox-terriers of undoubted pedigree and more than doubtful ownership, for Ortheris was an inveterate poacher and pre-eminent among a regiment of neat-handed dog-stealers.

Never again will the long lazy evenings return wherein Ortheris, whistling softly, moved surgeon-wise among the captives of his craft at the bottom of the well; when Learoyd sat in the niche, giving sage counsel on the management of "tykes," and Mulvaney, from the crook of the overhanging *pipal*, waved his enormous boots in benediction above our heads, delighting us with tales of Love and War, and strange experiences of cities and men.

Ortheris—landed at last in the "little stuff bird-shop" for which your soul longed; Learoyd—back again in the smoky, stone-ribbed North, amid the clang of the Bradford looms; Mulvaney—grizzled, tender and very wise Ulysses, sweltering on the earthwork of a Central India line—judge if I have forgotten old days in the Trap!

Orth'ris, as allus thinks he knaws more than other foaks, said she wasn't a real laady, but nobbut a Hewrasian. I don't gainsay as her culler was a bit doosky like. But she *was* a laady. Why, she rode iv a carriage, an' good 'osses too, an' her 'air was that oiled as you could see your faice in it, an' she wore dimond rings an' a goold chain, an' silk an' satin dresses as mun 'a cost a deal, for it isn't a cheap shop as keeps enough o' one pattern to fit a figure like hers. Her name was Mrs. DeSussa, an' t' waay I coom to be acquainted wi' her was along of our Colonel's Laady's dog Rip.

I've seen a vast o' dogs, but Rip was t' prettiest picter of a cliver fox-tarrier 'at iver I set eyes on. He could do owt you like but speeak, an' t' Colonel's Laady set more store by him than if he had been a Christian. She hed bairns of her awn, but they was i' England, and Rip seemed to get all t' coodlin' and pettin' as belonged to a bairn by good right.

But Rip were a bit on a rover, an' hed a habit o' breakin' out o' barricks like, and trottin' round t' plaice as if he were t' Cantonment Magistrate coom round inspectin'. The Colonel leathers him once or twice, but Rip didn't care an' kept on gooin' his rounds, wi' his taail a-waggin' as if he were flag-signallin' to t' world at large 'at he was " gettin' on nicely, thank yo, and how's yo'sen ? " An' then t' Colonel, as was noa sort of a hand wi' a dog, tees him oop. A real clipper of a dog, an' it's noa wonder yon laady, Mrs. DeSussa, should tek a fancy tiv him. Theer's one o' t' Ten Commandments says yo maun't cuvvet your neebor's ox nor his jackass, but it dosen't say nowt about his tarrier dogs, an' happen thot's t' reason why Mrs. DeSussa cuvveted Rip, tho' she went to church reg'lar along wi' her husband who was so mich darker 'at if he hedn't such a good coaat tiv' his back yo might ha' called him a black man and nut tell a lee nawther. They said he addled his brass i' jute, an' he'd a rare lot on it.

Well, you seen, when they teed Rip up, t' poor awd lad didn't enjoy very good 'elth. So t' Colonel's Laady sends for me as 'ad a naame for beiu' knowledgeable about a dog, an' axes what's ailin' wi' him.

"Why," says I, "he's getten t' mopes, an what he wants is his libbaty an' coompany like t' rest on us; wal happen a rat or two 'ud liven him oop. It's low, mum," says I, "is rats, but it's t' nature of a dog; an' soa's cuttin' round an' meetin' another dog or two an' passin' t' time o' day, an' hevvin' a bit of a turn-up wi' him like a Christian."

So she says *her* dog maunt niver fight an' noa Christians iver fought.

"Then, what's a soldier for?" says I; an' I explains to her t' contrairy qualities of a dog, 'at, when yo' coom to think on't, is one o' t' curusest things as is. For they larn to behave theirsens like gentlemen born, fit for t' fost o' coompany— they tell me t' Widdy herself is fond of a good dog and knaws one when she sees it as well as onny body : then on t'other hand a-tewin' round after cats an' gettin' mixed oop i' all manners o' blackguardly street rows, an' killin' rats, an' fightin' like divils.

T' Colonel's Laady says:—"Well, Learoyd, I doant agree wi' you, but you're right in a way o' speeakin, an' I should like yo' to tek Rip out a walkin' wi' you sometimes; but yo' maun't let him fight, nor chase cats, nor do nowt 'orrid ": an' them was her very wods.

Soa Rip an' me gooes out a' walkin' o' evenin's, he bein' a dog as did credit tiv' a man, an' I catches a lot o' rats an' we hed a bit of a match on in an awd dry swimmin' bath at back o' t' cantonments, an' it was none so long afore he was as bright as a button again. He hed a way o' flyin' at them big yaller pariah dogs as if he was a harrow offan a bow, an' though his weight were nowt, he tuk 'em so suddint-like they rolled over like skittles in a halley, an' when they coot he stretched after 'em as if he were rabbit-runnin'. Saame with cats when he cud get t' cat agaate o' runnin'.

One evenin', him an' me was trespassin' ovver a compound wall after one of them mungooses 'at he'd started, an' we was busy grubbin' round a prickle-bush, an' when we looks up there was Mrs. DeSussa wi' a parasel ovver her shoulder, a-watchin' us. "Oh my!" she sings out; "there's that lovelee dog! Would he let me stroke him, Mister Soldier?"

"Aye, he would, mum," sez I, "for he's fond o' laady's coompany. Coom here, Rip, an' speeak to this kind laady." An' Rip, seein' 'at t' mongoose hed getten clean awaay, cooms up like t' gentleman he was, nivver a hauporth shy nor okkord.

"Oh, you beautiful—you prettee dog!" she says, clippin' an' chantin' her speech in a way them sooart has o' their awn; "I would like a dog like you. You are so verree lovelee—so awfullee prettee," an' all thot sort o' talk, 'at a dog o' sense mebbe thinks nowt on, tho' he bides it by reason o' his breedin'.

An' then I meks him joomp ovver my swagger-cane, an' shek hands, an' beg, an' lie dead, an' a lot o' them tricks as laadies teeaches dogs, though I doan't haud with it mysen, for it's makin' a fool o' a good dog to do such like.

An' at lung length it cooms out 'at she'd been thrawin' sheep's eyes, as t' sayin' is, at Rip for many a day. Yo' see, her childer was grown up, an' she'd nowt mich to do an' were allus fond of a dog. Soa she axes me if I'd tek somethin' to dhrink. An' we goes into t' drawn-room wheer her 'usband was a-settin'. They meks a gurt fuss ovver t' dog an' I has a bottle o' aale an' he gave me a handful o' cigars.

Soa I coomed away, but t' awd lass sings out—"Oh, Mister Soldier, please coom again and bring that prettee dog".

I didn't let on to t' Colonel's Laady about Mrs. DeSussa, and Rip, he says nowt nawther; an' I gooes again, an' ivry time there was a good dhrink an' a handful o' good smooaks. An' I telled t' awd lass a heeap more about Rip than I'd ever heeared; how he tuk t' fost prize at Lunnon dog-show and cost thotty-three pounds fower shillin' from t' man as bred him; 'at his own brother was t' propputty o' t' Prince o'

Wailes, an' 'at he had a pedigree as long as a Dook's. An' she lapped it all oop an' were niver tired o' admirin' him. But when t' awd lass took to givin' me money an' I seed 'at she were gettin' fair fond about t' dog, I began to suspicion summat. Onny body may give a soldier t' price of a pint in a friendly way an' theer's no 'arm done, but when it cooms to five rupees slipt into your hand, sly like, why it's what t' 'lectioneerin' fellows calls bribery an' corruption. Specially when Mrs. DeSussa threwed hints how t' cold weather would soon be ovver an' she was goin' to Munsooree Pahar an' we was goin' to Rawalpindi, an' she would niver see Rip any more onless somebody she knowed on would be kind tiv her.

Soa I tells Mulvaney an' Ortheris all t' taale thro', beginnin' to end.

" 'Tis larceny that wicked ould laady manes," says t' Irishman, " 'tis felony she is sejuicin' ye into, my frind Learoyd, but I'll purtect your innocince. I'll save ye from the wicked wiles av that wealthy ould woman, an' I'll go wid ye this evenin' and spake to her the wurrds av truth an' honesty. But Jock," says he, waggin' his heead, " 'twas not like ye to kape all that good dhrink an' thim fine cigars to yerself, while Orth'ris here an' me have been prowlin' round wid throats as dry as lime-kilns, and nothin' to smoke but Canteen plug. 'Twas a dhirty thrick to play on a comrade, for why should you, Learoyd, be balancin' yourself on the butt av a satin chair, as if Terence Mulvaney was not the aquil av anybody who thrades in jute !"

"Let alone me," sticks in Orth'ris, " but that's like life. Them wot's really fitted to decorate society get no show while a blunderin' Yorkshireman like you ——"

"Nay," says I, "it's none o' t' blunderin' Yorkshireman she wants, it's Rip. He's t' gentleman this journey."

Soa t' next day, Mulvaney an' Rip an' me goes to Mrs. DeSussa's, an' t' Irishman bein' a strainger she wor a bit shy at fost. But yo've heeard Mulvaney talk, an' yo' may believe as he fairly bewitched t' awd lass wal she let out 'at she

wanted to tek Rip away wi' her to Munsooree Pahar.   Then
Mulvaney changes his tune an' axes her solemn-like if she'd
thought o' t' consequences o' gettin' two poor but honest
soldiers sent t' Andamning Islands.   Mrs. DeSussa began to
cry, so Mulvaney turns round oppen t' other tack and smooths
her down, allowin' 'at Rip ud be a vast better off in t' hills
than down i' Bengal, and 'twas a pity he shouldn't go wheer
he was so well beliked.   And soa he went on, backin' an'
fillin' an' workin' up t' awd lass wal she felt as if her life
warn't worth nowt if she didn't heve t' dog.

   Then all of a suddint he says :—" But ye *shall* have him,
marm, for I've a feelin' heart, not like this could-blooded
Yorkshireman ; but 'twill cost ye not a penny less than three
hundher rupees ".

   "Don't yo' believe him, mum," says I ; "t' Colonel's
Laady wouldn't tek five hundred for him."

   "Who said she would ?" says Mulvaney ; "it's not
buyin' him I mane, but for the sake o' this kind, good laady,
I'll do what I never dreamt to do in my life.   I'll stale him !"

   "Don't say steal," says Mrs. DeSussa ; "he shall have
the happiest home.   Dogs often get lost, you know, and then
they stray, an' he likes me and I like him as I niver liked
a dog yet, an' I *must* hev him.   If I got him at t' last minute
I could carry him off to Munsooree Pahar and nobody would
niver knaw."

   Now an' again Mulvaney looked acrost at me, an' though
I could mak nowt o' what he was after, I concluded to take
his leead.

   "Well, mum," I says, " I never thowt to coom down to
dog steealin', but if my comrade sees how it could be done to
oblige a laady like yo'sen, I'm nut t' man to hod back, tho'
it's a bad business I'm thinkin', an' three hundred rupees is a
poor set-off again t' chance of them Damning Islands as
Mulvaney talks on."

   "I'll mek it three fifty," says Mrs DeSussa ; "only let
me hev t' dog !"

So we let her persuade us, an' she teks Rip's measure theer an' then, an' sent to Hamilton's to order a silver collar again t' time when he was to be her awn, which was to be t' day she set off for Munsooree Pahar.

"Sitha, Mulvaney," says I, when we was outside, "you're niver goin' to let her hev Rip!"

"An' would ye disappoint a poor old woman?" says he; "she shall have *a* Rip."

"An' wheer's he to come through?" says I.

"Learoyd, my man," he sings out, "you're a pretty man av your inches an' a good comrade, but your head is made av duff. Isn't our friend Orth'ris a Taxidermist, an' a rale artist wid his nimble white fingers? An' what's a Taxidermist but a man who can thrate shkins? Do ye mind the white dog that belongs to the Canteen Sargint, bad cess to him—he that's lost half his time an' snarlin' the rest? He shall be lost for *good* now; an' do ye mind that he's the very spit in shape an' size av the Colonel's, barrin' that his tail is an inch too long, an' he has none av the colour that divarsifies the rale Rip, an' his timper is that av his masther an' worse. But fwhat is an inch on a dog's tail? An' fwhat to a professional like Orth'ris is a few ringstraked shpots av black, brown an' white? Nothin' at all, at all."

Then we meets Orth'ris, an' that little man bein' sharp as a needle, seed his way through t' business in a minute. An' he went to work a practisin' 'air-dyes the very next day, beginnin' on some white rabbits he had, an' then he drored all Rip's markin's on t' back of a white Commissariat bullock, so as to get his 'and in an' be sure of his colours; shadin' off brown into black as natral as life. If Rip *hed* a fault it was too mich markin', but it was straingely reg'lar, an' Orth'ris settled himself to make a fost-rate job on it when he got haud o' t' Canteen Sargint's dog. Theer niver was sich a dog as thot for bad temper, an' it did nut get no better when his tail hed to be fettled an inch an' a-half shorter. But they may talk o' theer Royal Academies as they like. *I* niver seed a bit o' animal paintin' to beat t' copy as Orth'ris made of Rip's marks, wal t' picter itself was snarlin' all t' time an' tryin' to get at Rip standin' theer to be copied as good as goold.

Orth'ris allus hed as mich conceit on himsen as would lift a balloon, an' he wor so pleeased wi' his sham Rip he wor for tekking him to Mrs. DeSussa before she went away. But Mulvaney an' me stopped thot, knowin' Orth'ris's work, though niver so cliver, was nobbut skin-deep.

An' at last Mrs. DeSussa fixed t' day for startin' to Munsooree Pahar. We was to tek Rip to t' stayshun i' a basket an' hand him ovver just when they was ready to start, an' then she'd give us t' brass—as was agreed upon.

An' my wod! It were high time she were off, for them 'air-dyes upon t' cur's back took a vast of paintin' to keep t' reet culler, tho' Orth'ris spent a matter o' seven rupees six annas i' t' best drooggist shops i' Calcutta.

An' t' Canteen Sargint was lookin' for 'is dog everywheer; an', wi' bein' tied up, t' beast's timper got waur nor ever.

It wor i' t' evenin' when t' train started thro' Howrah, an' we 'elped Mrs. DeSussa wi' about sixty boxes, an' then we gave her t' basket. Orth'ris, for pride av his work, axed us to let him coom along wi' us, an' he couldn't help liftin' t' lid an' showin' t' cur as he lay coiled oop.

"Oh!" says t' awd lass; "the beautee! How sweet he looks!" An' just then t' beauty snarled an' showed his teeth, so Mulvaney shuts down t' lid and says: "Ye'll be careful, marm, whin ye tek him out. He's disaccustomed to travelling by t' railway, an' he'll be sure to want his rale mistress an' his friend Learoyd, so ye'll make allowance for his feelings at fost."

She would do all thot an' more for the dear, good Rip, an' she would nut oppen t' basket till they were miles away, for fear anybody should recognise him, an' we were real good and kind soldier-men, we were, an' she honds me a bundle o' notes, an' then cooms up a few of her relations an' friends to say good-bye—not more than seventy-five there wasn't—an' we cuts away.

What coom to t' three hundred and fifty rupees? Thot's what I can scarcelins tell you, but we melted it. It was share an' share alike, for Mulvaney said: "If Learoyd got hold of Mrs. DeSussa first, sure 'twas I that remimbered the Sargint's dog just in the nick av time, an' Orth'ris was the artist av janius that made a work av art out av that ugly piece av ill-nature. Yet, by way av a thank-offerin' that I was not led into felony by that wicked ould woman, I'll send a thrifle to Father Victor for the poor people he's always beggin' for."

But me an' Orth'ris, he bein' Cockney an' I bein' pretty far north, did nut see it i' t' saame way. We'd getten t' brass an' we meaned to keep it. An' soa we did—for a short time.

Noa—noa, we niver heeard a wod more o' t' awd lass. Our rig'mint went to Pindi, an' t' Canteen Sargint he got himself another tyke insteead o' t' one 'at got lost so reg'lar an' was lost for good at last.

THE BIG DRUNK DRAF'.

We're goin' 'ome, we're goin' 'ome—
 Our ship is *at* the shore,
An' you mus' pack your 'aversack,
 For we won't come back no more.
Ho, don't you grieve for me,
 My lovely Mary Ann,
For I'll marry you yet on a fourp'ny bit,
 As a time-expired ma-a-an!

Barrack-room Ballad.

AN awful thing has happened! My friend Private Mulvaney, who went home in the *Serapis*, time-expired, not very long ago, has come back to India as a civilian! It was all Dinah Shadd's fault. She could not stand the poky little lodgings, and she missed her servant Abdullah more than words could tell. The fact was that the Mulvaneys had been out here too long, and had lost touch of England.

Mulvaney knew a contractor on one of the new Central India lines, and wrote to him for some sort of work. The contractor said that if Mulvaney could pay the passage he would give him command of a gang of coolies for old sake's sake. The pay was eighty-five rupees a month, and Dinah Shadd said that if Terence did not accept she would make his life a "basted purgathory". Therefore the Mulvaneys came out as "civilians," which was a great and terrible fall; though Mulvaney tried to disguise it by saying that he was "Ker'nel on the railway line, an' a consequinshal man".

He wrote me an invitation, on a tool-indent form, to visit him; and I came down to the funny little "construction" bungalow at the side of the line. Dinah Shadd had planted peas about and about, and nature had spread all

manner of green stuff round the place.   There was no change
in Mulvaney except the change of raiment, which was
deplorable, but could not be helped.   He was standing upon
his trolly, haranguing a gang-man, and his shoulders were as
well drilled, and his big, thick chin was as clean shaven as
ever.

" I'm a civilian now," said Mulvaney.   " Cud you tell that
I was iver a martial man ?   Don't answer, Sorr, av you're
strainin' betune a complimint an' a lie.   There's no houldin'
Dinah Shadd now she's got a house av her own.   Go inside
an' dhrink tay out av chiny in the drrrrawin' room, an' thin
we'll dhrink like Christians undher the tree here.   Scutt, ye
naygur-folk !   There's a *Sahib* come to call on me, an' that's
more than he'll iver do for you onless you run !   Get out,
an' go on pilin' up the earth, quick, till sundown."

When we three were comfortably settled under the big
sisham in front of the bungalow, and the first rush of
questions and answers about Privates Ortheris and Learoyd
and old times and places had died away, Mulvaney said,
reflectively :—" Glory be there's no p'rade to-morrow, an' no
bunheaded Corp'ril-bhoy to give you his lip.   An' yit I don't
know.   'Tis harrd to be something ye niver were an' niver
meant to be, an' all the ould days shut up along wid your
papers.   Eyah !   I'm growin' rusty, an' 'tis the will av God
that a man mustn't serve his Quane for time an' all."

He helped himself to a fresh peg and sighed furiously.

" Let your beard grow, Mulvaney," said I, " and then you
won't be troubled with those notions.   You'll be a real
civilian."

Dinah Shadd had confided to me, in the drawing-room,
her desire to coax Mulvaney into letting his beard grow.
" 'Twas so civilian-like," said poor Dinah, who hated her
husband's hankering for his old life.

" Dinah Shadd, you're a dishgrace to an honust, clane-
scraped man !" said Mulvaney, without replying to me.
Grow a beard on your own chin, darlint, and lave my

razors alone. They're all that stand betune me and dis-ris-pect-ability. Av I didn't shave, I wud be torminted wid an outrajis thurrst; for there's nothin' so dhryin' to the throat as a big billy-goat beard waggin' undher the chin. Ye wudn't have me dhrink *always*, Dinah Shadd? By the same token, you're kapin' me crool dhry now. Let me look at that whisky."

The whisky was lent and returned, but Dinah Shadd, who had been just as eager as her husband in asking after old friends, rent me with :—

"I take shame for you, Sorr, comin' down here—though the Saints know you're as welkim as the daylight whin you *do* come—an' upsettin' Terence's head wid your nonsense about—about fwhat's much better forgotten. He bein' a civilian now, an' you niver was aught else. Can you not let the Arrmy rest? 'Tis not good for Terence."

I took refuge by Mulvaney, for Dinah Shadd has a temper of her own.

"Let be—let be," said Mulvaney. "'Tis only wanst in a way I can talk about the ould days." Then to me :—"Ye say Dhrumshticks is well, an' his lady tu? I niver knew how I liked the grey garron till I was shut av' him an' Asia."—"Dhrumshtricks" was the nickname of the Colonel Commanding Mulvaney's old regiment.—"Will you be seein' him again? You will. Thin tell him"—Mulvaney's eyes began to twinkle—"tell him wid Privit ——"

"*Mister*, Terence," interrupted Dinah Shadd.

"Now the Divil an' all his angels an' the firmament av Hiven fly away wid the 'Mister,' an' the sin av makin' me swear be on your confession, Dinah Shadd! *Privit*, I tell ye. Wid *Privit* Mulvaney's best obedience, that but for me the last time-expired wud be still pullin' hair on their way to the sea."

He threw himself back in the chair, chuckled, and was silent.

"Mrs. Mulvaney," I said, "please take up the whisky, and don't let him have it until he has told the story."

Dinah Shadd dexterously whipped the bottle away, saying at the same time, " 'Tis nothing to be proud av," and thus captured by the enemy, Mulvaney spake :—

" 'Twas on Chuseday week. I was behaderin' round wid the gangs on the 'bankmint—I've taught the hoppers how to kape step an' stop screechin'—whin a head-gang-man comes up to me, wid about two inches av shirt-tail hangin round his neck an' a disthressful light in his oi. *'Sahib,'* sez he, 'there's a reg'mint an' a half av soldiers up at the junction, knockin' red cinders out av ivrything an' ivrybody! They thried to hang me in my cloth,' he sez, 'an' there will be murder an' ruin an' rape in the place before nightfall! They say they're comin' down here to wake us up. What will we do wid our women-folk ? '

" ' Fetch my throlly ! ' sez I ; 'my heart's sick in my ribs for a wink at anything wid the Quane's uniform on ut. Fetch my throlly, an' six av the jildiest men, and run me up in shtyle.' "

"He tuk his best coat," said Dinah Shadd, reproachfully.

" 'Twas to do honour to the Widdy. I cud ha' done no less, Dinah Shadd. You and your digresshins interfere wid the coorse av the narrative. Have you iver considhered fwhat I wud look like wid me *head* shaved as well as my chin ? You bear that in your mind, Dinah darlin'.

" I was throllied up six miles, all to get a shquint at that draf'. I *knew* 't was a spring draf' goin' home for there's no rig'mint hereabouts, more's the pity."

"Praise the Virgin ! " murmured Dinah Shadd. But Mulvaney did not hear.

"Whin I was about three-quarters av a mile off the rest-camp, powtherin' along fit to burrst, I heard the noise av the men, an', on my sowl, Sorr, I cud catch the voice av Peg Barney bellowin' like a bison wid the belly‑ache. You remimber Peg Barney that was in D Comp'ny—a red, hairy scraun, wid a scar on his jaw ? Peg Barney that cleared

3

out the Blue Lights' Jubilee meeting wid the cook-room mop
last year?

"Thin I knew ut was a draf' of the ould rig'mint, an'
I was conshumed wid sorrow for the bhoy that was in charge.
We was harrd scrapin's at any time. Did I iver tell you
how Horker Kelly wint into clink nakid as Phœbus Apol-
lonius, wid the shirts av the Corp'ril an' file undher his
arrum? An' *he* was a moild man! But I'm digreshin'.
'Tis a shame both to the rig'mints and the Arrmy sendin'
down little orf'cer bhoys wid a draf' av strong men mad wid
liquor an' the chanst av gettin' shut av India, an' *niver a
punishment that's fit to be given right down an' away from
cantonmints to the dock!* 'Tis this nonsince. Whin I am
servin' my time, I'm undher the Articles av War, an' can be
whipped on the peg for *thim*. But whin I've *served* my time,
I'm a Reserve man, an' the Articles av War haven't any
hould on me. An orf'cer *can't* do anythin' to a time-expired
savin' confinin' him to barricks. 'Tis a wise rig'lation
bekaze a time-expired does *not* have any barricks; bein' on
the move all the time. 'Tis a Solomon av a rig'lation, is that.
I wud like to be inthroduced to the man who secreted ut.
'Tis easier to get colts from a Kibbereen horse-fair into
Galway than to take a bad draf' over ten miles av country.
Consiquintly that rig'lation—for fear that the men wud be
hurt by the little orf'cer bhoy. No matther. The nearer my
throlly came to the rest-camp, the woilder was the shine, an'
the louder was the voice av Peg Barney. ''Tis good I am here,'
thinks I to myself, 'for Peg alone is employmint to two or
three.' He bein' I well knew, as copped as a dhrover.

"Faith, that rest-camp was a sight! The tent-ropes was
all skew-nosed, an' the pegs looked as dhrunk as the men—
fifty av thim—the scourin's, an' rinsin's, an' Divil's lavin's av
the Ould Rig'mint. I tell you, Sorr, they were dhrunker
than any men you've ever seen in your mortial life. *How*
does a draf' get dhrunk? How does a frog get fat? They
suk ut in through their shkins.

" There was Peg Barney sittin' on the groun' in his shirt—
wan shoe off an' wan shoe on—whackin' a tent-peg over the
head wid his boot, an' singin' fit to wake the dead. 'Twas
no clane song that he sung, though. 'Twas the Divil's Mass."

" What's that ? " I asked.

" Whin a bad egg is shut av the Army, he sings the
Divil's Mass for a good riddance; an' that manes swearin' at
ivrything from the Commandher-in-Chief down to the Room-
Corp'ril, such as you niver in your days heard. Some men
can swear so as to make green turf crack! Have you iver
heard the Curse in an Orange Lodge? The Divil's Mass is
ten times worse, an' Peg Barney was singin' ut, whackin' the
tent-peg on the head wid his boot for each man that he
cursed. A powerful big voice had Peg Barney, an' a hard
swearer he was whin sober. I stood forninst him, an' 'twas
not me oi alone that cud tell Peg was dhrunk as a coot.

" ' Good mornin', Peg,' I sez, whin he dhrew breath afther
cursin' the Adj'tint-Gen'ral; ' I've put on my best coat to see
you, Peg Barney,' sez I.

" ' Thin take ut off again,' sez Peg Barney, latherin' away
wid the boot; ' take ut off an' dance, ye lousy civilian ! '

" Wid that he begins cursin' ould Dhrumshticks, being so
full he clean misremimbers the Brigade-Major an' the Judge
Advokit Gen'ral.

" ' Do you not know me, Peg ? ' sez I, though me blood
was hot in me wid being called a civilian."

" An' him a decent married man ! " wailed Dinah Shadd.

" ' I do not,' sez Peg, ' but dhrunk or sober I'll tear the
hide off your back wid a shovel whin I've stopped singin'.'

" ' Say you so, Peg Barney ? ' sez I. ' 'Tis clear as mud
you've forgotten me. I'll assist your autobiography.' Wid
that I stretched Peg Barney, boot an' all, an' wint into the
camp. An awful sight ut was !

" ' Where's the orf'cer in charge av the detachmint ? '
sez I to Scrub Greene—the manest little worm that ever
walked.

"'There's no orf'cer, ye ould cook,' sez Scrub; 'we're a bloomin' Republic.'

"'Are you that?' sez I; 'thin I'm O'Connell the Dictator, an' by this you will larn to kape a civil tongue in your rag-box.'

"Wid that I stretched Scrub Greene an' wint to the orf'cer's tent. 'Twas a new little bhoy—not wan I'd iver seen before. He was sittin' in his tent, purtendin' not to 'ave ear av the racket.

"I saluted—but for the life av me I mint to shake hands whin I went in. 'Twas the sword hangin' on the tent-pole changed my will.

"'Can't I help, Sorr?' sez I; ''tis a strong man's job they've given you, an' you'll be wantin' help by sundown.' He was a bhoy wid bowils, that child, an' a rale gintleman.

"'Sit down,' sez he.

"'Not before my orf'cer,' sez I; an' I tould him fwhat my service was.

"'I've heard av you,' sez he. 'You tuk the town av Lungtungpen nakid.'

"'Faith,' thinks I, 'that's Honour an' Glory;' for 'twas Lift'nint Brazenose did that job. 'I'm wid ye, Sorr,' sez I, 'if I'm av use. They shud niver ha' sent you down wid the draf'. Savin' your presince, Sorr,' I sez, ''tis only Lift'nint Hackerston in the Ould Rig'mint can manage a Home draf'.'

"'I've niver had charge of men like this before,' sez he, playin' wid the pens on the table; 'an' I see by the Rig'lations ——'

"'Shut your oi to the Rig'lations, Sorr,' I sez, 'till the throoper's into blue wather. By the Rig'lations you've got to tuck thim up for the night, or they'll be runnin' foul av my coolies an' makin' a shiverarium half through the country. Can you trust your non-coms, Sorr?'

"'Yes,' sez he.

"'Good,' sez I; 'there'll be throuble before the night. Are you marchin', Sorr?'

" 'To the next station,' sez he.

" 'Better still,' sez I; 'there'll be big throuble.'

" 'Can't be too hard on a Home draf',' sez he; 'the great thing is to get thim in-ship.'

" 'Faith you've larnt the half av your lesson, Sorr,' sez I, 'but av you shtick to the Rig'lations you'll niver get thim in-ship at all, at all. Or there won't be a rag av kit betune thim whin you do.'

" 'Twas a dear little orf'cer bhoy, an' by way av kapin' his heart up, I tould him fwhat I saw wanst in a draf' in Egypt."

" What was that, Mulvaney?" said I.

" Sivin an' fifty men sittin' on the bank av a canal, laughin' at a poor little squidgereen av an orf'cer that they'd made wade into the slush an' pitch the things out av the boats for their Lord High Mightinesses. That made me orf'cer bhoy woild wid indignation.

" 'Soft an' aisy, Sorr,' sez I; 'you've niver had your draf' in hand since you left cantonmints. Wait till the night, an' your work will be ready to you. Wid your permission, Sorr, I will investigate the camp, an' talk to my ould frinds. 'Tis no manner av use thryin' to shtop the divilmint *now*.'

" Wid that I wint out into the camp an' inthrojuced my-silf to ivry man sober enough to remimber me. I was some wan in the ould days, an' the bhoys was glad to see me—all excipt Peg Barney wid a eye like a tomata five days in the bazar, an' a nose to correspon'. They come round me an' shuk me, an' I tould thim I was in privit employ wid an in-come av me own, an' a drrrawin'-room fit to bate the Quane's; an' wid me lies an' me shtories an' nonsinse gin'rally, I kept 'em quiet, in wan way an' another, knockin' roun' the camp. 'Twas *bad* even thin whin I was the Angil av Peace.

" I talked to me ould non-coms—*they* was sober—an' betune me an' thim we wore the draf' over into their tents at the proper time. The little orf'cer bhoy he comes round, decint an' civil-spoken as might be.

" 'Rough quarters, men,' sez he, 'but you can't look to be

as comfortable as in barricks. We must make the best av
things. I've shut my eyes to a dale av dog's trick to-day,
an' now there must be no more av ut.'

"'No more we will. Come an' have a dhrink, me son,'
sez Peg Barney, staggerin' where he stud. Me little orf'cer
bhoy kep' his timper.

"'You're a sulky swine, you are,' sez Peg Barney, an' at
that the men in the tent began to laugh.

"I tould you me orf'cer bhoy had bowils. He cut Peg
Barney as near as might be on the oi that I'd squshed whin
we first met. Peg wint spinnin' acrost the tent.

"'Peg him out, Sorr,' sez I, in a whishper.

"'Peg him out!' sez me orf'cer bhoy, up loud, just as if
'twas battalion-p'rade an' he pickin' his wurrds from the
Sargint.

"The non-coms tuk Peg Barney—a howlin' handful he
was—an' in three minuts he was pegged out—chin down,
tight-dhrawn—on his stummick, a peg to each arm an' leg,
swearin' fit to turn a naygur white.

"I tuk a peg an' jammed ut into his ugly jaw.—'Bite on
that, Peg Barney,' I sez; 'the night is settin' frosty, an'
you'll be wantin' diversion before the mornin'. But for the
Rig'lations you'd be bitin' on a bullet now at the thriangles,
Peg Barney,' sez I.

"All the draf' was out av their tents watchin' Barney
bein' pegged.

"''Tis agin the Rig'lations! He strook him!' screeches
out Scrub Greene, who was always a lawyer; an' some of the
men tuk up the shoutin'.

"'Peg out that man!' sez my orf'cer bhoy niver losin'
his timper; an' the non-coms wint in and pegged out Scrub
Greene by the side av Peg Barney.

"I cud see that the draf' was comin' roun'. The men
stud not knowin' fwhat to do.

"'Get to your tents!' sez me orf'cer bhoy. 'Sargint, put
a sintry over these two men.'

"The men wint back into the tents like jackals, an' the rest av the night there was no noise at all excipt the stip av the sintry over the two, an' Scrub Greene blubberin' like a child. 'Twas a chilly night, an' faith, ut sobered Peg Barney.

"Just before Revelly, my orf'cer bhoy comes out an' sez : 'Loose those men an' send thim to their tents!' Scrub Greene wint away widout a word, but Peg Barney, stiff wid the cowld, stud like a sheep, thryin' to make his orf'cer understhand he was sorry for playin' the goat.

"There was no tucker in the draf' whin ut fell in for the march, an' divil a wurrd about 'illegality' cud I hear.

"I wint to the ould Colour Sargint and I sez :—'Let me die in glory,' sez I. 'I've seen a man this day !'

"'A man he is,' sez ould Hother; 'the draf's as sick as a herrin'. They'll all go down to the sea like lambs. That bhoy has the bowils av a cantonmint av Gin'rals.'

"'Amin,' sez I, 'an' good luck go wid him, wheriver he be, by land or by sea. Let me know how the draf' gets clear.'

"An' do you know how they *did?* That bhoy, so I was tould by letter from Bombay, bullydamned 'em down to the dock, till they cudn't call their sowls their own. From the time they left me oi till they was 'tween decks, not wan av thim was more than dacintly dhrunk. An', by the Holy Articles av War, whin they wint aboard they cheered him till they cudn't spake, an' *that*, mark you, has not come about wid a draf' in the mim'ry av livin' man ! You look to that little orf'cer bhoy. He has bowils. 'Tis not ivry child that wud chuck the Rig'lations to Flanders an' stretch Peg Barney on a wink from a brokin an' dilapidated ould carkiss like mesilf. I'd be proud to serve —— "

"Terence, you're a civilian," said Dinah Shadd warningly.

"So I am—so I am. Is ut likely I wud forget ut ? But he was a gran' bhoy all the same, an' I'm only a mudtipper wid a hod on my shoulthers. The whisky's in the heel av your hand, Sorr. Wid your good lave we'll dhrink to the Ould Rig'mint—three fingers—standin' up ! "

And we drank.

THE SOLID MULDOON.

Did ye see John Malone, wid his shinin', brand-new hat?
Did ye see how he walked like a grand aristocrat?
There was flags an' banners wavin' high, an' dhress and
 shtyle were shown,
But the best av all the company was Misther John Malone.

—John Malone.

THIS befel in the old days and, as my friend Private
 Mulvaney was specially careful to make clear, the
Unregenerate.

There had been a royal dog-fight in the ravine at the
back of the rifle-butts, between Learoyd's *Jock* and Ortheris's
Blue Rot—both mongrel Rampur hounds, chiefly ribs and
teeth. It lasted for twenty happy, howling minutes, and
then *Blue Rot* collapsed and Ortheris paid Learoyd three
rupees, and we were all very thirsty. A dog-fight is a most
heating entertainment, quite apart from the shouting, because
Rampurs fight over a couple of acres of ground. Later, when
the sound of belt-badges clinking against the necks of beer-
bottles had died away, conversation drifted from dog to man-
fights of all kinds. Humans resemble red-deer in some
respects. Any talk of fighting seems to wake up a sort of
imp in their breasts, and they bell one to the other, exactly
like challenging bucks. This is noticeable even in men who
consider themselves superior to Privates of the Line: it
shows the Refining Influence of Civilization and the March
of Progress.

Tale provoked tale, and each tale more beer. Even
dreamy Learoyd's eyes began to brighten, and he unburdened
himself of a long history in which a trip to Malham Cove, a

girl at Pateley Brigg, a ganger, himself and a pair of clogs were mixed in drawling tangle.

"An' so Ah coot's yead oppen from t' chin to t' hair, an' he was abed for t' matter o' a month," concluded Learoyd, pensively.

Mulvaney came out of a reverie—he was lying down—and flourished his heels in the air. "You're a man, Learoyd," said he critically, "but you've only fought wid men, an' that's an ivry-day expayrience; but I've stud up to a ghost, an' that was *not* an ivry-day expayrience."

"No?" said Ortheris, throwing a cork at him. "You git up an' address the 'ouse—you an' yer expayriences. Is it a bigger one nor usual?"

"'Twas the livin' trut'!" answered Mulvaney, stretching out a huge arm and catching Ortheris by the collar. "Now where are ye, me son? Will ye take the wurrud av the Lorrd out av my mouth another time?" He shook him to emphasize the question.

"No, somethin' else, though," said Ortheris, making a dash at Mulvaney's pipe, capturing it and holding it at arm's length; "I'll chuck it acrost the ditch if you don't let me go!"

"You maraudin' hathen! 'Tis the only cutty I iver loved. Handle her tinder or I'll chuck *you* acrost the nullah. If that poipe was bruk—— Ah! Give her back to me, Sorr!"

Ortheris had passed the treasure to my hand. It was an absolutely perfect clay, as shiny as the black ball at Pool. I took it reverently, but I was firm.

"Will you tell us about the ghost-fight if I do?" I said.

"Is ut the shtory that's troublin' you? Av course I will. I mint to all along. I was only gettin' at ut my own way, as Popp Doggle said whin they found him thryin' to ram a cartridge down the muzzle. Orth'ris, fall away!"

He released the little Londoner, took back his pipe, filled it, and his eyes twinkled. He has the most eloquent eyes of any one that I know.

"Did I iver tell you," he began, "that I was wanst the divil av a man?"

"You did," said Learoyd with a childish gravity that made Ortheris yell with laughter, for Mulvaney was always impressing upon us his merits in the old days.

"Did I iver tell you," Mulvaney continued calmly, "that I was wanst more av a divil than I am now?"

"Mer—ria! You don't mean it?" said Ortheris.

"Whin I was Corp'ril—I was rejuced aftherwards—but, as I say, *whin* I was Corp'ril, I was a divil of a man."

He was silent for nearly a minute, while his mind rummaged among old memories and his eye glowed. He bit upon the pipe-stem and charged into his tale.

"Eyah! They was great times. I'm ould now; me hide's wore off in patches; sinthry-go has disconceited me, an' I'm a married man tu. But I've had my day, I've had my day, an' nothin' can take away the taste av that! Oh my time past, whin I put me fut through ivry livin' wan av the Tin Commandmints between Revelly and Lights Out, blew the froth off a pewter, wiped me mustache wid the back av me hand, an' slept on ut all as quiet as a little child! But ut's over—ut's over, an' 'twill niver come back to me; not though I prayed for a week av Sundays. Was there *any* wan in the Ould Rig'mint to touch Corp'ril Terence Mulvaney whin that same was turned out for sedukshin? I niver met him. Ivry woman that was not a witch was worth the runnin' afther in those days, an' ivry man was my dearest frind or ——I had stripped to him an' we knew which was the betther av the tu.

"Whin I was Corp'ril I wud not ha' changed wid the Colonel—no, nor yet the Commandher-in-Chief. I wud be a Sargint. There was nothin' I wud not be! Mother av Hivin, look at me! Fwhat am I *now?* But no matther! I must get to the other ghosts—not the wans in my ould head.

"We was quartered in a big cantonmint—'tis no manner av use namin' names, for ut might give the barricks disrepitation—an' I was the Imperor av the Earth to my own mind, an' wan or tu women thought the same. Small blame to thim. Afther we had lain there a year, Bragin, the Colour Sargint av E Comp'ny, wint an' took a wife that was lady's maid to some big lady in the Station. She's dead now is Annie Bragin—died in child-bed at Kirpa Tal, or ut may ha' been Almorah—seven—nine years gone, an' Bragin he married agin. But she was a pretty woman whin Bragin inthrojuced her to cantonmint society. She had eyes like the brown av a buttherfly's wing whin the sun catches ut, an' a waist no thicker than my arm, an' a little sof' button av a mouth I wud ha' gone through all Asia bristlin' wid bay'nits to get the kiss av. An' her hair was as long as the tail av the Colonel's charger—forgive me mintionin' that blunderin' baste in the same mouthful with Annie Bragin—but 'twas all shpun gold, an' time was whin a lock av ut was more than di'monds to me. There was niver pretty woman yet, an' I've had thruck wid a few, cud open the door to Annie Bragin.

" 'Twas in the Carth'lic Chapel I saw her first, me oi rolling round as usual to see fwhat was to be seen. 'You're too good for Bragin, my love,' thinks I to mesilf, 'but that's a mistake I can put straight, or my name is not Terence Mulvaney.'

"Now take my wurrd for ut, you Orth'ris there an' Learoyd, an' kape out av the Married Quarters—as I did not. No good iver comes av ut, an' there's always the chance av your bein' found wid your face in the dirt, a long picket in the back av your head, an' your hands playing the fifes on the tread av another man's doorstep. 'Twas so we found O'Hara, he that Rafferty killed six years gone, when he wint to his death wid his hair oiled, whistlin' *Larry O'Rourke* betune his teeth. Kape out av the Married Quarters, I say, as I did not. 'Tis onwholesim, 'tis dangerous, an' 'tis ivrything else that's bad, but——O my sowl, 'tis swate while ut lasts !

" I was always hangin' about there whin I was off duty an'

Bragin wasn't, but niver a sweet word beyon' ordinar' did I get from Annie Bragin. ' 'Tis the pervarsity av the sect,' sez I to mesilf, an' gave my cap another cock on my head an' straightened my back—'twas the back av a Dhrum Major in those days—an' wint off as tho' I did not care, wid all the women in the Married Quarters laughin'. I was pershuaded —most bhoys *are* I'm thinkin'—that no woman born av woman cud stand against me av I hild up me little finger. I had reason for thinkin' that way—till I met Annie Bragin.

"Time an' agin whin I was blandandherin' in the dusk a man wud go past me as quiet as a cat. ' That's quare,' thinks I, ' for I am, or I should be, the only man in these parts. Now what divilment can Annie be up to ? ' Thin I called myself a blayguard for thinkin' such things ; but I thought thim all the same. An' that, mark you, is the way av a man.

"Wan evenin' I said :—' Mrs. Bragin, manin' no dis-respect to you, who is that Corp'ril man'—I had seen the stripes though I cud niver get sight av his face—' *who* is that Corp'ril man that comes in always whin I'm goin' away ? '

"' Mother av God ! ' sez she, turnin' as white as my belt; ' have *you* seen him too ? '

"' Seen him ! ' sez I ; ' av coorse I have. Did ye want me not to see him, for '—we were standin' talkin' in the dhark, outside the verandah av Bragin's quarters—' you'd betther tell me to shut me eyes. Onless I'm mistaken, he's come now.'

"An', sure enough, the Corp'ril man was walkin' to us, hangin' his head down as though he was ashamed av himsilf.

"' Good-night, Mrs. Bragin,' sez I, very cool ; ' 'tis not for me to interfere wid your *a-moors;* but you might manage these things wid more dacincy. I'm off to canteen,' I sez.

"I turned on my heel an' wint away, swearin' I wud give that man a dhressin' that wud shtop him messin' about the Married Quarters for a month an' a week. I had not tuk ten paces before Annie Bragin was hangin' on to my arm, an' I cud feel that she was shakin' all over.

" ' Stay wid me, Mister Mulvaney ! ' sez she ; ' you're flesh an' blood, at the least—are ye not ? '

" ' I'm *all* that,' sez I, an' my anger wint away in a flash. ' Will I want to be asked twice, Annie ? '

" Wid that I slipped my arm round her waist, for, begad, I fancied she had surrindered at discretion, an' the honours av war were mine.

" ' Fwhat nonsinse is this ? ' sez she, dhrawin' hersilf up on the tips av her dear little toes. ' Wid the mother's milk not dhry on your impident mouth ! Let go ! ' she sez.

" ' Did ye not say just now that I was flesh and blood ? ' sez I. ' I have not changed since,' I sez ; an' I kep' my arm where ut was.

" ' Your arms to yoursilf ! ' sez she, an' her eyes sparkild.

" ' Sure, 'tis only human nature,' sez I ; an' I kep' my arm where ut was.

" ' Nature or no nature,' sez she, ' you take your arm away or I'll tell Bragin, an' he'll alter the nature av your head. Fwhat d'you take me for ? ' she sez.

" ' A woman,' sez I ; ' the prettiest in barricks.'

" ' A *wife*,' sez she ; ' the straightest in cantonmints ! '

" Wid that I dropped my arm, fell back tu paces, an' saluted, for I saw that she mint fwhat she said."

" Then you know something that some men would give a good deal to be certain of. How could you tell ? " I demanded in the interests of Science.

" ' Watch the hand,' said Mulvaney ; ' av she shuts her hand tight, thumb down over the knuckle, take up your hat an' go. You'll only make a fool av yoursilf av you shtay. But av the hand lies opin on the lap, or av you see her thryin' to shut ut an' she can't,—go on ! She's not past reasonin' wid.'

" Well, as I was sayin' I fell back, saluted, an' was goin' away.

" ' Shtay wid me,' she sez. ' Look ! He's comin' again.'

" She pointed to the verandah, an', by the Hoight av Impart'nince, the Corp'ril man was comin' out av Bragin's quarters!

"'He's done that these five evenin's past,' sez Annie Bragin. 'O, fwhat will I do!'

"'He'll not do ut again," sez I, for I was fightin' mad.

"Kape away from a man that has been a thrifle crossed in love till the fever's died down. He rages like a brute beast.

"I wint up to the man in the verandah, manin', as sure as I sit, to knock the life out av him. He slipped into the open. 'Fwhat are you doin' philanderin' about here, ye scum av the gutter?' sez I polite, to give him his warnin', for I wanted him ready.

"He niver lifted his head, but sez, all mournful an' melancolius, as if he thought I wud be sorry for him : 'I can't find her,' sez he.

"'My troth,' sez I, 'you've lived too long—you an' your seekin's an' findin's in a dacint married woman's quarters! Hould up your head, ye frozen thief av Genesis,' sez I, 'an' you'll find all you want an' more!'

"But he niver hild up, an' I let go from the shoulder to where the hair is short over the eyebrows.

"'That'll do your business,' sez I, but it nearly did mine instid. I put my body-weight behind the blow, but I hit nothin' at all, an' near put my shoulther out. The Corp'ril man was not there, an' Annie Bragin, who had been watchin' from the verandah, throws up her heels an' carries on like a cock whin his neck's wrung by the dhrummer-bhoy. I wint back to her, for a livin' woman, an' a woman like Annie Bragin, is more than a p'rade-groun' full av ghosts. I'd never seen a woman faint before, an' I stud like a shtuck calf, askin' her whether she was dead, an' prayin' her for the love av me, an' the love av her husband, an' the love av the Virgin, to opin her blessed eyes again, an' callin' mesilf all the names undher the canopy av Hivin for plaguin' her wid my miserable *a-moors* whin I ought to ha' stud betune her an' this Corp'ril man that had lost the number av his mess.

"I misremimber fwhat nonsinse I said, but I was not so far gone that I cud not hear a fut on the dirt outside. 'Twas Bragin comin' in, an' by the same token Annie was comin' to. I jumped to the far end av the verandah an' looked as if butter wudn't melt in my mouth. But Mrs. Quinn, the Quarter Master's wife that was, had tould Bragin about my hangin' round Annie.

"'I'm not pleased wid you, Mulvaney,' sez Bragin, unbucklin' his sword, for he had been on duty.

"'That's bad hearin',' I sez, an' I knew that the pickets were dhriven in. 'What for, Sargint?' sez I.

"'Come outside,' sez he, 'an' I'll show you why.'

"'I'm willin',' I sez; 'but my stripes are none so ould that I can afford to lose thim. Tell me now, *who* do I go out wid?' sez I.

"He was a quick man an' a just, an' saw fwhat I wud be afther. 'Wid Mrs. Bragin's husband,' sez he. He might ha' known by me askin' that favour that I had done him no wrong.

"We wint to the back av the arsenal an' I stripped to him, an' for ten minutes 'twas all I cud do to prevent him killin' himself against my fistes. He was mad as a dumb dog—just frothing wid rage; but he had no chanst wid me in reach, or learnin', or anything else.

"'Will ye hear reason?' sez I, whin his first wind was runnin' out.

"'Not whoile I can see,' sez he. Wid that I gave him both, one after the other, smash through the low gyard that he'd been taught whin he was a boy, an' the eyebrow shut down on the cheekbone like the wing av a sick crow.

"'Will you hear reason now, ye brave man?' sez I.

"'Not whoile I can speak,' sez he, staggerin' up blind as a stump. I was loth to do ut, but I wint round an' swung into the jaw side-on an' shifted ut a half pace to the lef'.

"'Will ye hear reason now?' sez I; 'I can't keep my timper much longer, an' 'tis like I will hurt you.'

" ' Not whoile I can stand,' he mumbles out av one corner av his mouth.   So I closed an' threw him—blind, dumb, an' sick, an' jammed the jaw straight.

" ' Your're an ould fool, *Mister* Bragin,' sez I.

" ' You're a young thief,' sez he, ' an' you've bruk my heart, you an' Annie betune you! '

" Thin he began cryin' like a child as he lay.   I was sorry as I had niver been before.   'Tis an awful thing to see a strong man cry.

" ' I'll swear on the Cross! ' sez I.

" ' I care for none av your oaths,' sez he.

" ' Come back to your quarters,' sez I, ' an' if you don't believe the livin', begad, you shall listen to the dead,' I sez.

" I hoisted him an' tuk him back to his quarters.   ' Mrs. Bragin,' sez I, ' here's a man that you can cure quicker than me.'

" ' You've shamed me before my wife,' he whimpers.

" ' Have I so? ' sez I.   ' By the look on Mrs. Bragin's face I think I'm for a dhressin'-down worse than I gave you.'

" An' I was!   Annie Bragin was woild wid indignation. There was not a name that a dacint woman cud use that was not given my way.   I've had my Colonel walk roun' me like a cooper roun' a cask for fifteen minuts in Ord'ly Room, bekaze I wint into the Corner Shop an unstrapped lewnatic, but all that I iver tuk from his rasp av a tongue was ginger-pop to fwhat Annie tould me.   An' that, mark you, is the way av a woman.

" Whin ut was done for want av breath, an' Annie was bendin' over her husband, I sez: ' 'Tis all thrue, an' I'm a blayguard an' you're an honest woman ; but will you tell him of wan service that I did you? '

" As I finished speakin' the Corp'ril man came up to the verandah, an' Annie Bragin shquealed.   The moon was up, an' we cud see his face.

" ' I can't find her,' sez the Corp'ril man, an' wint out like the puff av a candle.

" Saints stand betune us an' evil !' sez Bragin, crossin' himself ; 'that's Flahy av the Tyrone Rig'mint.'

" 'Who was he ?' I sez, ' for he has given me a dale av fightin' this day.'

" Bragin tould us that Flahy was a Corp'ril who lost his wife av cholera in those quarters three years gone, an' wint mad, an' *walked* afther they buried him, huntin' for her.

" ' Well,' sez I to Bragin, ' he's been hookin' out av Purgathory to kape company wid Mrs. Bragin ivry evenin' for the last fortnight. You may tell Mrs. Quinn, wid my love, for I know that she's been talkin to you, an' you've been listenin', that she ought to ondherstand the differ 'twixt a man an' a ghost. She's had three husbands,' sez I, ' an' *you*'ve got a wife too good for you. Instid av which you lave her to be boddered by ghosts an'—an' all manner av evil spirruts. I'll niver go talkin' in the way av politeness to a man's wife again. Good-night to you both,' sez I ; an' wid that I wint away, havin' fought wid woman, man and Divil all in the heart av an hour. By the same token I gave Father Victor wan rupee to say a mass for Flahy's soul, me havin' discommoded him by shticking my fist into his systim."

" Your ideas of politeness seem rather large, Mulvaney," I said.

" That's as you look at ut," said Mulvaney calmly ; " Annie Bragin niver cared for me. For all that, I did not want to leave anything behin' me that Bragin could take hould av to be angry wid her about—whin an honust wurrd cud ha' cleared all up. There's nothing like opin-speakin'. Orth'ris, ye scutt, let me put me oi to that bottle, for my throat's as dhry as whin I thought I wud get a kiss from Annie Bragin. An' that's fourteen years gone ! Eyah ! Cork's own city an' the blue sky above ut —— an' the times that was—the times that was ! "

4

WITH THE MAIN GUARD.

Der jungere Uhlanen
Sit round mit open mouth
While Breitmann tell dem stdories
Of fightin' in the South ;
Und gif dem moral lessons,
How before der battle pops,
Take a little prayer to Himmel
Und a goot long drink of Schnapps.
—*Hans Breitmann's Ballads.*

"MARY, Mother av Mercy, fwhat the divil possist us to take an' kape this melancolious counthry? Answer me that, Sorr."

It was Mulvaney who was speaking. The hour was one o'clock of a stifling hot June night, and the place was the main gate of Fort Amara, most desolate and least desirable of all fortresses in India. What I was doing there at that hour is a question which only concerns McGrath the Sergeant of the Guard, and the men on the gate.

"Slape," said Mulvaney, "is a shuparfluous necessity. This gyard 'll shtay lively till relieved." He himself was stripped to the waist; Learoyd on the next bedstead was dripping from the skinful of water which Ortheris, arrayed only in white trousers, had just sluiced over his shoulders; and a fourth private was muttering uneasily as he dozed open-mouthed in the glare of the great guard-lantern. The heat under the bricked archway was terrifying.

"The worrst night that iver I remimber. Eyah! Is all Hell loose this tide?" said Mulvaney. A puff of burning wind lashed through the wicket-gate like a wave of the sea and Ortheris swore.

"Are ye more heasy, Jock?" he said to Learoyd. "Put yer 'ead between your legs. It'll go orf in a minute."

"Ah don't care. Ah would not care, but ma heart is plaayin' tivvy-tivvy on ma ribs. Let me die! Oh leave

' Put yer 'ead between your legs.   It'll go orf in a minute.'

me die!" groaned the huge Yorkshireman, who was feeling the heat acutely, being of fleshly build.

The sleeper under the lantern roused for a moment and raised himself on his elbow.—" Die and be damned then !' he said. "*I*'m damned and I can't die !"

" Who's that ? " I whispered, for the voice was new to me.

" Gentleman born," said Mulvaney ; " Corp'ril wan year Sargint nex'. Redhot on his C'mission, but dhrinks like a fish. He'll be gone before the cowld weather's here. So ! "

He slipped his boot, and with the naked toe just touched the trigger of his Martini. Ortheris misunderstood the movement, and the next instant the Irishman's rifle was dashed aside, while Ortheris stood before him, his eyes blazing with reproof.

" You !" said Ortheris. " My Gawd, *you !* If it was you, wot would *we* do ? "

" Kape quiet, little man," said Mulvaney, putting him aside, but very gently ; " 'tis not me, nor will ut be me whoile Dinah Shadd's here. I was but showin' something."

Learoyd, bowed on his bedstead, groaned, and the gentleman ranker sighed in his sleep. Ortheris took Mulvaney's tendered pouch, and we three smoked gravely for a space while the dust-devils danced on the glacis and scoured the red-hot plain without.

" Pop ? " said Ortheris, wiping his forehead.

"Don't tantalize wid talkin' av dhrink, or I'll shtuff you into your own breech-block an'—fire you off ! " grunted Mulvaney.

Ortheris chuckled, and from a niche in the verandah produced six bottles of gingerade.

" Where did ye get ut, ye Machiavel ? " said Mulvaney, " 'Tis no bazar pop."

" 'Ow do *Hi* know wot the Orf'cers drink ? " answered Ortheris. " Arst the mess-man."

" Ye'll have a Disthrict Coort-martial settin' on ye yet, me son," said Mulvaney, "but"—he opened a bottle—"I will not report ye this time. Fwhat's in the mess-kid is mint for the belly, as they say, 'specially whin that mate is dhrink. Here's

luck! A bloody war or a —— no, we've got the sickly
season. War, thin!"—he waved the innocent "pop" to the
four quarters of Heaven. "Bloody war! North, East, South,
an' West! Jock, ye quakin' hayrick, come an' dhrink."

But Learoyd, half mad with the fear of death presaged in
the swelling veins of his neck, was imploring his Maker to
strike him dead, and fighting for more air between his
prayers. A second time Ortheris drenched the quivering
body with water and the giant revived.

"An Ah divn't see thot a mon is i' fettle for gooin' on to
live; an Ah divn't see thot there is owt for t' livin' for.
Hear now, lads! Ah'm tired—tired. There's nobbut watter
i' ma bones. Let me die!"

The hollow of the arch gave back Learoyd's broken
whisper in a bass boom. Mulvaney looked at me hope-
lessly, but I remembered how the madness of despair had
once fallen upon Ortheris, that weary, weary afternoon in the
banks of the Khemi River, and how it had been exorcised by
the skilful magician Mulvaney.

"Talk, Terence!" I said, "or we shall have Learoyd
slinging loose, and he'll be worse than Ortheris was. Talk!
He'll answer to your voice."

Almost before Ortheris had deftly thrown all the rifles of
the Guard on Mulvaney's bedstead, the Irishman's voice was
uplifted as that of one in the middle of a story, and turning
to me, he said:—

"In barricks or out of it, as *you* say, Sorr, an Oirish rig'mint
is the divil an' more. 'Tis only fit for a young man wid
eddicated fisteses. O the crame av disruption is an Oirish
rig'mint, an' rippin', tearin', ragin' scattherers in the field av
war! My first rig'mint was Oirish—Faynians an' rebils to
the heart av their marrow was they, an' *so* they fought for the
Widdy betther than most, bein' contrairy—Oirish. They was
the Black Tyrone. You've heard av thim, Sorr?"

Heard of them! I knew the Black Tyrone for the choicest
collection of unmitigated blackguards, dogstealers, robbers of

hen-roosts, assaulters of innocent citizens and recklessly daring heroes in the Army List. Half Europe and half Asia has had cause to know the Black Tyrone—good luck be with their tattered Colours as Glory has ever been !

"They *was* hot pickils an' ginger ! I cut a man's head tu deep wid my belt in the days av my youth, an', afther some circumstances which I will oblitherate, I came to the Ould Rig'mint, bearin' the character av a man wid hands an' feet. But, as I was goin' to tell you, I fell acrost the Black Tyrone agin wan day whin we wanted thim powerful bad. Orth'ris, me son, fwhat was the name av that place where they sint wan comp'ny av us an' wan av the Tyrone roun' a hill an' down again, all for to tache the Paythans something they'd niver learned before ? Afther Ghuzni 'twas."

"Don't know what the bloomin' Paythans called it. We called it Silver's Theayter. You know that, sure ! "

"Silver's Theatre—so 'twas. A gut betune two hills, as black as a bucket, an' as thin as a gurl's waist. There was overmany Paythans for our convaynience in the gut, an' begad they called thimselves a Reserve—bein' impident by natur ! Our Scotchies an' lashins av Gurkys was poundin' into some Paythan rig'ments, I think 'twas. Scotchies an' Gurkys are twins bekaze they're so onlike, an' they get dhrunk together whin God plases. Well, as I was sayin', they sint wan comp'ny av the Ould an wan av the Tyrone to double up the hill an' clane out the Paythan Reserve. Orf'cers was scarce in thim days, fwhat wid dysintry an' not takin' care av thimselves, an' we was sint out wid only wan orf'cer for the comp'ny ; but he was a Man that had his feet beneath him, an' all his teeth in their sockuts."

"Who was he ? " I asked.

"Captain O'Neil—Old Crook—Cruik-na-bulleen—him that I tould ye that tale av whin he was in Burma. Hah ! He was a Man. The Tyrone tuk a little orf'cer bhoy, but divil a bit was he in command, as I'll dimonstrate presintly. We an' they came over the brow av the hill, wan on each side av the gut, an' there was that ondacint Reserve waitin' down below like rats in a pit.

" ' Howld on, men,' sez Crook, who tuk a mother's care av us always. ' Rowl some rocks on thim by way av visitin'-kyards.' We hadn't rowled more than twinty bowlders, an' the Paythans was beginnin' to swear tremenjus, whin the little orf'cer bhoy av the Tyrone shqueaks out acrost the valley :—' Fwhat the devil an' all are you doin', shpoilin' the fun for my men ? Do ye not see they'll stand ? '

" ' Faith, that's a rare pluckt wan !' sez Crook. ' Niver mind the rocks, men. Come along down an' take tay wid thim ! '

" ' There's damned little sugar in ut ! ' sez my rear-rank man ; but Crook heard.

" ' Have ye not all got spoons ? ' he sez, laughin', an' down we wint as fast as we cud. Learoyd bein' sick at the Base, he, av coorse, was not there."

" Thot's a lie ! " said Learoyd, dragging his bedstead nearer. " Ah gotten *thot* theer, an' you knaw it, Mulvaney." He threw up his arms, and from the right arm-pit ran, diagonally through the fell of his chest, a thin white line terminating near the fourth left rib.

" My mind's goin'," said Mulvaney, the unabashed. " Ye were there. Fwhat I was thinkin' of ! 'Twas another man, av coorse. Well, you'll remimber thin, Jock, how we an' the Tyrone met wid a bang at the bottom an' got jammed past all movin' among the Paythans."

" Ow ! It *wos* a tight 'ole. Hi was squeeged till I thought I'd bloomin' well bust," said Ortheris, rubbing his stomach meditatively.

" 'Twas no place for a little man, but *wan* little man "—Mulvaney put his hand on Ortheris's shoulder—" saved the life av me. There we shtuck, for divil a bit did the Paythans flinch, an' divil a bit dare we ; our business bein' to clear 'em out. An' the most exthryordinar' thing av all was that we an' they just rushed into each others' arrums, an' there was no firing for a long time. Nothin' but knife an bay'nit when we cud get our hands free:

that was not often. We was breast on to thim, an' the Tyrone was yelpin' behind av us in a way I didn't see the lean av at first. But I knew later, an' so did the Paythans.

" ' Knee to knee ! ' sings out Crook, wid a laugh whin the rush av our comin' into the gut shtopped, an' he was huggin' a hairy great Paythan, neither bein' able to do anything to the other, tho' both was wishful.

" ' Breast to breast ! ' he says, as the Tyrone was pushin' us forward closer an' closer.

" 'An' hand over back ! ' sez a Sargint that was behin'. I saw a sword lick out past Crook's ear like a snake's tongue, an' the Paythan was tuk in the apple av his throat like a pig at Dromeen fair.

" ' Thank ye, Brother Inner Guard,' sez Crook, cool as a cucumber widout salt. ' I wanted that room.' An' he wint forward by the thickness av a man's body, havin' turned the Paythan undher him. The man bit the heel off Crook's boot in his death-bite.

" ' Push, men ! ' sez Crook. ' Push, ye paper-backed beggars ! ' he sez. ' Am I to pull ye through ? ' So we pushed, an' we kicked, an' we swung, an' we swore, an' the grass bein' slippery, our heels wouldn't bite, an' God help the front-rank man that wint down that day ! ' "

" 'Ave you ever bin in the Pit hentrance o' the Vic. on a thick night ? " interrupted Ortheris. " It was worse nor that, for they was goin' one way, an' we wouldn't 'ave it. Leastaways, Hi 'adn't much to say."

" Faith, me son, ye said ut, thin. I kep' the little man betune my knees as long as I cud, but he was pokin' roun' wid his bay'nit, blindin' an' stiffin' feroshus. The devil of a man is Orth'ris in a ruction—aren't ye ? " said Mulvaney.

" Don't make game ! " said the Cockney. " I knowed I wasn't no good then, but I guv 'em compot from the lef' flank when we opened out. No ! " he said, bringing down his hand with a thump on the bedstead, " a bay'nit ain't no good to a little man—might as well 'ave a bloomin' fishin' rod! I 'ate a clawin'. maulin' mess, but gimme a breech that's wore out a bit, an' hamminition one year in store, to let the powder kiss the bullet, an' put me somewheres where I ain't trod on by 'ulkin swine like you, an' s'elp me Gawd, I could bowl you over five times outer seven at height 'undred. Would yer try, you lumberin' Hirishman?"

"No, ye wasp. I've seen ye do ut. I say there's nothin' better than the bay'nit, wid a long reach, a double twist av ye can, an' a slow recover."

"Dom the bay'nit," said Learoyd, who had been listening intently. "Look a-here!" He picked up a rifle an inch below the foresight with an underhanded action, and used it exactly as a man would use a dagger.

"Sitha," said he softly, "thot's better than owt, for a mon can bash t' faace wi' thot, an, if he divn't, he can breeak t' fore-arm o' t' gaard. 'Tis not i' t' books, though. Gie me t' butt."

"Each does ut his own way, like makin' love," said Mulvaney quietly; "the butt or the bay'nit or the bullet accordin' to the natur' av the man. Well, as I was sayin', we shtuck there breathin' in each other's faces an' swearin' powerful; Orth'ris cursin' the mother that bore him bekaze he was not three inches taller.

"Prisintly he sez:—'Duck, ye lump, an' I can get at a man over your shouldher!'

"'You'll blow me head off,' I sez, throwin' my arm clear; 'go through under my arm-pit, ye bloodthirsty little scutt,' sez I, 'but don't shtick me or I'll wring your ears round.'"

"Fwhat was ut ye gave the Paythan man forninst me, him that cut at me whin I cudn't move hand or foot? Hot or cowld was ut?"

"Cold," said Ortheris, "up an' under the rib-jint. 'E come down flat. Best for you 'e did."

"Thrue, my son! This jam thing that I'm talkin' about lasted for five minutes good, an' thin we got our arms clear an' wint in. I misremimber exactly fwhat I did, but I didn't want Dinah to be a widdy at the Depôt. Thin, after some

'He ran forward wid the Haymakers' Lift on his bay'nit.'

promishkuous hackin', we shtuck again, an' tne Tyrone behin'
was callin' us dogs an' cowards an' all manner av names ; we
barrin' their way.

"'Fwhat ails the Tyrone ?' thinks I ; 'they've the makin's
av a most convanient fight here.'

"A man behind me sez beseechful an' in a whisper :—' Let
me get at thim ! For the Love av Mary give me room beside
ye, ye tall man !'

"'An' who are you that's so anxious to be kilt ?' sez I,
widout turnin' my head, for the long knives was dancin' in
front like the sun on Donegal Bay whin ut's rough.

"'We've seen our dead,' he sez, squeezin' into me ; 'our
dead that was men two days gone ! An' me that was his
cousin by blood could not bring Tim Coulan off ! Let me get
on,' he sez, ' let me get to thim or I'll run ye through the back !'

"'My troth,' thinks I, 'if the Tyrone have seen their dead,
God help the Paythans this day !' An' thin I knew why the
Oirish was ragin' behind us as they was.

"I gave room to the man, an' he ran forward wid the Haymakers' Lift on his bay'nit an' swung a Paythan clear off his
feet by the belly-band av the brute, an' the iron bruk at the
lockin'-ring.

"'Tim Coulan 'll slape easy to-night,' sez he wid a grin ;
an' the next minut his head was in two halves and he wint
down grinnin' by sections.

"The Tyrone was pushin' an' pushin' in, an' our men was
swearin' at thim, an' Crook was workin' away in front av us
all, his sword-arm swingin' like a pump-handle an' his revolver
spittin' like a cat. But the strange thing av ut was the quiet
that lay upon. 'Twas like a fight in a drame—excipt for
thim that was dead.

"Whin I gave room to the Oirishman I was expinded an'
forlorn in my inside. 'Tis a way I have, savin' your presince,
Sorr, in action. ' Let me out, bhoys,' sez I, backin' in among
thim. ' I'm goin' to be onwell !' Faith they gave me room at
the wurrud, though they would not ha' given room for all Hell

wid the chill off. When I got clear, I was, savin' your presince, Sorr, outragis sick bekaze I had dhrunk heavy that day.

" Well an' far out av harm was a Sargint av the Tyrone sittin' on the little orf'cer bhoy who had stopped Crook from rowlin' the rocks. O he was a beautiful bhoy, an' the long black curses was sliding out av his innocint mouth like mornin'-jew from a rose !

" ' Fwhat have you got there ? ' sez I to the Sargint.

" ' Wan av Her Majesty's bantams wid his spurs up,' sez he. ' He's goin' to Coort-martial me.'

" ' Let me go ! ' sez the little orf'cer bhoy. ' Let me go and command my men ! ' manin' thereby the Black Tyrone which was beyond any command—ay, even av they had made the Divil a Field-orf'cer.

" ' His father howlds my mother's cow-feed in Clonmel,' sez the man that was sittin' on him. ' Will I go back to *his* mother an' tell her that I've let him throw himself away ? Lie still, ye little pinch av dynamite, an' Coort-martial me aftherwards.'

" ' Good,' sez I ; ' 'tis the likes av him makes the likes av the Commandher-in-Chief, but we must presarve thim. Fwhat d' you want to do, Sorr ? ' sez I, very politeful.

" ' Kill the beggars—kill the beggars ! ' he shqueaks ; his big blue eyes fairly brimmin' wid tears.

" ' An' how'll ye do that ? ' sez I. ' You've shquibbed off your revolver like a child wid a cracker ; you can make no play wid that fine large sword av yours ; an' your hand's shakin' like an asp on a leaf. Lie still and grow,' sez I.

" ' Get back to your comp'ny,' sez he ; ' you're insolint !'

" ' All in good time,' sez I, ' but I'll have a dhrink first.'

" Just thin Crook comes up, blue an' white all over where he wasn't red.

" ' Wather ! ' sez he ; 'I'm dead wid drouth ! O, but it's a gran' day ! '

" He dhrank half a skinful, and the rest he tilts into his chest, an' it fair hissed on the hairy hide av him. He sees the little orf'cer bhoy undher the Sargint.

" ' Fwhat's yonder ? ' sez he.

" 'Mutiny, Sorr,' sez the Sargint, an' the orf'cer bhoy begins pleadin' pitiful to Crook to be let go : but divil a bit wud Crook budge.

" ' Kape him there,' he sez, ' 'tis no child's work this day. By the same token,' sez he, ' I'll confishcate that iligant nickel-plated scent-sprinkler av yours, for my own has been vomitin' dishgraceful ! '

" The fork av his hand was black wid the back-spit av the machine. So he tuk the orf'cer bhoy's revolver. Ye may look, Sorr, but, by my faith, *there's a dale more done in the field than iver gets into Field Ordhers !*

" ' Come on, Mulvaney,' sez Crook ; 'is this a Coort-martial ? ' The two av us wint back together into the mess an' the Paythans were still standin' up. They was not *too* impart'nint though, for the Tyrone was callin' wan to another to remimber Tim Coulan.

" Crook stopped outside av the strife an' looked anxious, his eyes rowlin' roun'.

" ' Fwhat is ut, Sorr ? ' sez I ; ' can I get ye anything ? '

" ' Where's a bugler ? ' sez he.

" I wint into the crowd—our men was dhrawin' breath behin' the Tyrone who was fightin' like sowls in tormint—an' prisintly I came acrost little Frehan, our bugler bhoy, pokin' roun' among the best wid a rifle an' bay'nit.

" ' Is amusin' yoursilf fwhat you're paid for, ye limb ? ' sez I, catchin' him by the scruff. ' Come out av that an' attind to your duty,' I sez ; but the bhoy was not pleased.

" ' I've got wan,' sez he, grinnin', 'big as you, Mulvaney, an' fair half as ugly. Let me go get another.'

" I was dishpleased at the personability av that remark, so I tucks him under my arm an' carries him to Crook who was watchin' how the fight wint. Crook cuffs him till the bhoy cries, an' thin sez nothin' for a whoile.

" The Paythans began to flicker onaisy, an' our men roared. ' Opin ordher ! Double ! ' sez Crook. ' Blow, child, blow for the honour av the British Arrmy ! '

"That bhoy blew like a typhoon, an' the Tyrone an' we opined out as the Paythans broke, an' I saw that fwhat had gone before wud be kissin' an' huggin' to fwhat was to come. We'd dhruv thim into a broad part av the gut whin they gave, an' thin' we opined out an' fair danced down the valley, dhrivin' thim before us.   O 'twas lovely, an' stiddy too !   There was the Sargints on the flanks av what was left av us, kapin' touch, an' the fire was runnin' from flank to flank, an' the Paythans was dhroppin'.   We opined out wid the widenin' av the valley, an' whin the valley narrowed we closed again like the shticks on a lady's fan, an' at the far ind av the gut where they thried to stand, we fair blew them off their feet, for we had expinded very little ammunition by reason av the knife work."

"Hi used thirty rounds goin' down that valley," said Ortheris, "an' it was gentleman's work.   Might a done it in a white 'and-kerchief an' pink silk stockin's, that part.   Hi was on in that piece."

"You could ha' heard the Tyrone yellin' a mile away," said Mulvaney, "an' 'twas all their Sargints cud do to get thim off.   They was mad—mad—mad !   Crook sits down in the quiet that fell whin we had gone down the valley, an' covers his face wid his hands.   Prisintly we all came back again accordin' to our natures and disposhins, for they, mark you, show through the hide av a man in that hour.

"'Bhoys ! bhoys !' sez Crook to himself.   'I misdoubt we cud ha' engaged at long range an' saved betther men than me.'   He looked at our dead an' said no more.

"'Captain dear,' sez a man av the Tyrone, comin' up wid his mouth bigger than iver his mother kissed ut, spittin' blood like a whale ; 'Captain dear,' sez he, 'if wan or two in the shtalls have been discommoded, the gallery have enjoyed the performinces av a Roshus.'

"Thin I knew that man for the Dublin dock-rat he was— wan av the bhoys that made the lessee av Silver's Theatre grey before his time wid tearin' out the bowils av the benches an' t'rowin' thim into the pit.   So I passed the wurrud that I knew when I was in the Tyrone an' we lay in Dublin.   'I

don't know who 'twas,' I whispers, 'an' I don't care, but anyways I'll knock the face av you, Tim Kelly.'

"'Eyah!' sez the man, 'was you there too? We'll call
ut Silver's Theatre.' Half the Tyrone, knowin' the ould place,
tuk ut up : so we called ut Silver's Theatre.

"The little orf'cer bhoy av the Tyrone was thrimblin' an'
cryin'. He had no heart for the Coort Martials that he talked
so big upon. 'Ye'll do well later,' sez Crook, very quiet, 'for
not bein' allowed to kill yourself for amusemint.'

"'I'm a dishgraced man!' sez the little orf'cer bhoy.

"'Put me undher arrest, Sorr, if you will, but, by my sowl, I'd
do ut again sooner than face your mother wid you dead,' sez the
Sargint that had sat on his head, standin' to attention an' salutin'.
But the young wan only cried as tho' his little heart was breakin'.

"Thin another man av the Tyrone came up, wid the fog
av fightin' on him."

"The what, Mulvaney?"

"Fog av fightin'. You know, Sorr, that, like makin' love,
ut takes each man diff'rint. Now I can't help bein' powerful
sick whin I'm in action. Orth'ris, here, niver stops swearin'
from ind to ind, an' the only time that Learoyd opins his
mouth to sing is whin he is messin' wid other people's heads;
for he's a dhirty fighter is Jock Learoyd. Recruities sometime cry, an' sometime they don't know fwhat they do, an'
sometime they are all for cuttin' throats an' such like dirtiness ; but some men get heavy-dead-dhrunk on the fightin'.
This man was. He was staggerin', an' his eyes were half-
shut, an' we cud hear him dhraw breath twinty yards away.
He sees the little orf'cer bhoy, an' comes up, talkin' thick an'
drowsy to himsilf. 'Blood the young whelp!' he sez; 'blood
the young whelp!' an' wid that he threw up his arms, shpun
roun', an' dropped at our feet, dead as a Paythan, an' there
was niver sign or scratch on him. They said 'twas his heart
was rotten, but O 'twas a quare thing to see!

"Thin we wint to bury our dead, for we wud not lave
thim to the Paythans, an' in movin' among the haythen we
nearly lost that little orf'cer bhoy. He was for givin' wan

divil wather and layin' him aisy against a rock. 'Be careful,
Sorr,' sez I; 'a wounded Paythan's worse than a live wan.'
My troth, before the words was out of my mouth, the man
on the ground fires at the orf'cer bhoy lanin' over him, an' I
saw the helmit fly. I dropped the butt on the face av the
man an' tuk his pistol. The little orf'cer bhoy turned very
white, for the hair av half his head was singed away.

  "'I tould you so, Sorr!' sez I; an', afther that, whin he
wanted to help a Paythan I stud wid the muzzle contagious
to the ear. They dare not do anythin' but curse. The
Tyrone was growlin' like dogs over a bone that has been
taken away too soon, for they had seen their dead an' they
wanted to kill ivry sowl on the ground. Crook tould thim that
he'd blow the hide off any man that misconducted himself; but,
seeing that ut was the first time the Tyrone had iver seen their
dead, I do not wondher they were on the sharp. 'Tis a shame-
ful sight! Whin I first saw ut I wud niver ha' given quarter
to any man north of the Khaibar—no, nor woman either,
for the women used to come out afther dhark—— Auggrh!

  " Well, evenshually we buried our dead an' tuk away our
wounded, an' come over the brow av the hills to see the
Scotchies an' the Gurkys taking tay with the Paythans in
bucketsfuls. We were a gang av dissolute ruffians, for the
blood had caked the dust, an' the sweat had cut the cake, an'
our bay'nits was hangin' like butchers' steels betune ur legs,
an' most av us were marked one way or another.

  " A Staff Orf'cer man, clean as a new rifle, rides up an'
sez :—' What damned scarecrows are you ?'

  "'A comp'ny av Her Majesty's Black Tyrone an' wan
av the Ould Rig'mint,' sez Crook very quiet, givin' our
visitors the flure as 't was.

  "'Oh!' sez the Staff Orf'cer; 'did you dislodge that Reserve?'
  "'No!' sez Crook, an' the Tyrone laughed.
  "'Thin fwhat the divil have ye done?'
  "'Disthroyed ut,' sez Crook, an' he took us on, but not
before Toomey that was in the Tyrone sez aloud his

voice somewhere in his stummick :—'Fwhat in the name
av misfortune does this parrit widout a tail mane by
shtoppin' the road av his betthers ?'

"The Staff Orf'cer wint blue, an' Toomey makes him
pink by changin' to the voice av a minowderin' woman an'
sayin' :—' Come an' kiss me, Major dear, for me husband's
at the wars an' I'm all alone at the Depôt.'

"The Staff Orf'cer wint away, an' I cud see Crook's
sheulthers shakin'.

"His Corp'ril checks Toomey. 'Lave me alone,' sez Toomey,
widout a wink. 'I was his bâtman before he was married an'
he knows fwhat I mane, av you don't. There's nothin' like livin
in the hoight av society.' D'you remimber that, Orth'ris !"

"Hi do. Toomey, 'e died in 'orspital, next week it was,
'cause I bought 'arf his kit ; an' I remember after that——"

"GUARRD, TURN OUT !"

The Relief had come : it was four o'clock. "I'll catch a
kyart for you, Sorr," said Mulvaney, diving hastily into his
accoutrements. "Come up to the top av the Fort an' we'll
pershue our invistigations into McGrath's shtable." The
relieved Guard strolled round the main bastion on its way
to the swimming-bath, and Learoyd grew almost talkative.
Ortheris looked into the Fort ditch and across the plain.
"Ho ! it's weary waitin' for Ma-ary !" he hummed ; "but
I'd like to kill some more bloomin' Paythans before my
time's up. War ! Bloody war ! North, East, South, and West."

"Amen," said Learoyd slowly.

"Fwhat's here?" said Mulvaney, checking at a blur of white
by the foot of the old sentry-box. He stooped and touched it.
"It's Norah—Norah McTaggart ! Why, Nonie darlin', fwhat
are ye doin' out av your mother's bed at this time ?"

The two-year old child of Sergeant McTaggart must
have wandered for a breath of cool air to the very verge
of the parapet of the Fort ditch. Her tiny night-shift
was gathered into a wisp round her neck and she moaned
in her sleep. "See there !" said Mulvaney ; "poor lamb
Look at the heat-rash on the innocint skin av her. 'Tis

hard—crool hard even for us. Fwhat must it be for
these? Wake up, Nonie, your mother will be woild about
you. Begad, the child might ha' fallen into the ditch!"

He picked her up in the growing light, and set her on his
shoulder, and her fair curls touched the grizzled stubble of his
temples. Ortheris and Learoyd followed snapping their fingers,
while Norah smiled at them a sleepy smile. Then carolled
Mulvaney, clear as a lark, dancing the baby on his arm :—

> "If any young man should marry you,
> Say nothin' about the joke ;
> That iver ye slep' in a sinthry-box,
> Wrapped up in a soldier's cloak ".

"Though, on my sowl, Nonie," he said gravely, "there was
not much cloak about you. Niver mind, you won't dhress
like this ten years to come. Kiss your friends an' run along
to your mother."

Nonie, set down close to the Married Quarters, nodded
with the quiet obedience of the soldier's child, but, ere she
pattered off over the flagged path, held up her lips to be
kissed by the Three Musketeers. Ortheris wiped his mouth
with the back of his hand and swore sentimentally ; Learoyd
turned pink ; and the two walked away together. The
Yorkshireman lifted up his voice and gave in thunder the
chorus of *The Sentry-box,* while Ortheris piped at his side.

" 'Bin to a bloomin' sing-song, you two ? " said the Artil-
leryman, who was taking his cartridge down to the Morning
Gun. "You're over merry for these dashed days."

> "I bid ye take care o' the brat, said he,
> For it comes of a noble race,"

bellowed Learoyd. The voices died out in the swimming bath.

"Oh, Terence!" I said, dropping into Mulvaney's speech,
when we were alone, "it's you that have the Tongue!"

He looked at me wearily ; his eyes were sunk in his head,
and his face was drawn and white. "Eyah!" said he ; "I've
blandandhered thim through the night some how, but can thim
that helps others help thimselves ? Answer me that, Sorr!

And over the bastions of Fort Amara broke the pitiless day.

He picked her up in the growing light, and set her on his shoulder

THE 'EATHEN

THE 'eathen in 'is blindness bows down to wood an'
    stone;
'E don't obey no orders unless they is 'is own;
'E keeps 'is side-arms awful: 'e leaves 'em all about,
An' then comes up the regiment an' pokes the
    'eathen out.

> *All along o' dirtiness, all along o' mess,*
> *All along o' doin' things rather-more-or-less,*
> *All along of abby-nay,[1] kul,[2] an' hazar-ho,[3]*
> *Mind you keep your rifle an' yourself jus' so!*

The young recruit is 'aughty—'e draf's from Gawd
    knows where;
They bid 'im show 'is stockin's an' lay 'is mattress
    square;

---

[1] Not now.   [2] To-morrow.   [3] Wait a bit.

'E calls it bloomin' nonsense—'e doesn't know, no
    more—
An' then up comes 'is Company an' kicks 'im round
    the floor !

The young recruit is 'ammered—'e takes it very 'ard;
'E 'angs 'is 'ead an' mutters—'e sulks about the
    yard ;
'E talks o' ' cruel tyrants ' 'e 'll swing for by-an'-by,
An' the others 'ears an' mocks 'im, an' the boy goes
    orf to cry.

The young recruit is silly—'e thinks o' suicide ;
'E's lost 'is gutter-devil ; 'e 'asn't got 'is pride ;
But day by day they kicks 'im, which 'elps 'im on
    a bit,
Till e' finds 'isself one mornin' with a full an' proper
    kit.

Gettin' clear o' dirtiness, gettin' done with mess,
Gettin' shut o' doin' things rather-more-or-less ;
Not so fond of abby-nay, kul, nor hazar-ho,
Learns to keep 'is rifle an' 'isself jus' so !

The young recruit is 'appy—'e throws a chest to suit;
You see 'im grow mustaches; you 'ear 'im slap 'is
boot;
'E learns to drop the 'bloodies' from every word 'e
slings,
An' 'e shows an 'ealthy brisket when 'e strips for bars
an' rings.

The cruel-tyrant-sergeants they watch 'im 'arf a
year;
They watch 'im with 'is comrades, they watch 'im
with 'is beer;
They watch 'im with the women at the regimental
dance,
And the cruel-tyrant-sergeants send 'is name along
for ' Lance.'

An' now 'e 's 'arf o' nothin', an' all a private yet,
'Is room they up an' rags 'im to see what they will
get;
They rags 'im low an' cunnin', each dirty trick they
can,
But 'e learns to sweat 'is temper an' e' learns to
sweat 'is man.

An', last, a Colour-Sergeant, as such to be obeyed,
'E schools 'is men at cricket, 'e tells 'em on parade;
They sees 'em quick an' 'andy, uncommon set an'
    smart,
An' so 'e talks to orficers which 'ave the Core at
    'eart.

'E learns to do 'is watchin' without it showin' plain;
'E learns to save a dummy, an' shove 'im straight
    again;
'E learns to check a ranker that's buyin' leave to
    shirk;
An' 'e learns to make men like 'im so they'll learn
    to like their work.

An' when it comes to marchin' he'll see their socks
    are right,
An' when it comes to action 'e shows 'em 'ow to
    sight;
'E knows their ways of thinkin' and just what's in
    their mind;
'E knows when they are takin' on an' when they've
    fell be'ind.

'E knows each talkin' corpril that leads a squad
    astray ;
'E feels 'is innards 'eavin', 'is bowels givin' way ;
'E sees the blue-white faces all tryin' 'ard to grin,
An' 'e stands an' waits an' suffers till it's time to
    cap 'em in.

An' now the hugly bullets come peckin' through
    the dust,
An' no one wants to face 'em, but every beggar
    must ;
So, like a man in irons which isn't glad to go,
They moves 'em off by companies uncommon stiff
    an' slow.

Of all 'is five years' schoolin' they don't remember
    much
Excep' the not retreatin', the step an' keepin'
    touch.
It looks like teachin' wasted when they duck an'
    spread an' 'op,
But if 'e 'adn't learned 'em they'd be all about the
    shop !

An' now it's ''Oo goes backward?' an' now it's
    ''Oo comes on?'
And now it's 'Get the doolies,' an' now the
    captain's gone;
An' now it's bloody murder, but all the while they
    'ear
'Is voice, the same as barrick drill, a-shepherdin' the
    rear.

'E's just as sick as they are, 'is 'eart is like to split,
But 'e works 'em, works 'em, works 'em till he feels
    'em take the bit;
The rest is 'oldin' steady till the watchful bugles
    play,
An' 'e lifts 'em, lifts 'em, lifts 'em through the
    charge that wins the day!

The 'eathen in 'is blindness bows down to wood an'
    stone;
'E don't obey no orders unless they is 'is own;
The 'eathen in 'is blindness must end where 'e began,
But the backbone of the Army is the non-commissioned
    man!

Keep away from dirtiness—keep away from mess.
Don't get into doin' things rather-more-or-less !
Let's ha' done with abby-nay, kul, an' hazar-ho ;
Mind you keep your rifle an' yourself jus' so !

IN THE MATTER OF A PRIVATE.

Hurrah ! hurrah ! a soldier's life for me !
Shout boys, shout ! for it makes you jolly and free.
                                    —*The Ramrod Corps.*

PEOPLE who have seen, state that one of the quaintest spectacles of human frailty is an outbreak of hysterics in a girls' school. It starts without warning, generally on a hot afternoon, among the elder pupils. A girl giggles till the giggle gets beyond control. Then she throws up her head, and cries "*Honk, honk, honk,*" like a wild goose, and tears mix with the laughter. If the mistress be wise, she will say something severe at this point to check matters. If she be tender-hearted and send for a drink of water, the chances are largely in favour of another girl laughing at the afflicted one and herself collapsing. Thus the trouble spreads, and may end in half of what answers to the Lower Sixth of a boys' school rocking and whooping together. Given a week of warm weather, two stately promenades per diem, a heavy mutton and rice meal in the middle of the day, a certain amount of nagging from the teachers, and a few other things, some really amazing effects can be secured. At least, this is what folk say who have had experience.

Now, the Mother Superior of a Convent and the Colonel of a British Infantry Regiment would be justly shocked at any comparison being made between their respectives charges. But it is a fact that, under certain circumstances, Thomas in bulk can be worked up into ditthering, rippling hysteria. He does not weep, but he shows his trouble unmistakably, and the consequences get into the newspapers, and all the good and virtuous people who hardly know a Martini from a Snider say: "Take away the brute's ammunition !"

5

Thomas isn't a brute, and his business, which is to look after the virtuous people, demands that he shall have his ammunition to his hand. He doesn't wear silk stockings, and he really ought to be supplied with a new Adjective to help him to express his opinions : but, for all that, he is a great man. If you call him "the heroic defender of the national honour" one day, and "a brutal and licentious soldiery" the next, you naturally bewilder him, and he looks upon you with suspicion. There is nobody to speak for Thomas except people who have theories to work off on him ; and nobody understands Thomas except Thomas, and he does not know what is the matter with himself.

That is the prologue. This is the story :—

Corporal Slane was engaged to be married to Miss Jhansi McKenna, whose history is well known in the regiment and elsewhere. He had secured his Colonel's leave, and, being popular with the men, every arrangement had been made to give the wedding what Private Ortheris called "eeklar". It fell in the heart of the hot weather, and after the wedding, Slane was going up to the Hills with the bride. None the less, Slane's grievance was that the affair would be only a hired carriage wedding, and he felt that the "eeklar" of that was meagre. Miss McKenna did not care so much. The Sergeant's wife was helping her to make her wedding-dress, and she was very busy. Slane was, just then, the only moderately contented man in barracks. All the rest were more or less miserable.

And they had so much to make them happy, too! All their work was over at eight in the morning, and for the rest of the day they could lie on their backs and smoke Canteen plug and swear at the punkah-coolies. They enjoyed a fine, full flesh meal in the middle of the day, and then threw themselves down on their cots and sweated and slept till it was cool enough to go out with their "towny," whose vocabulary contained less than six hundred words, and the Adjective, and whose views on every conceivable question they had heard many months before.

There was the Canteen of course, and there was the Temperance room with the second-hand papers in it ; but a man of any profession cannot read for eight hours a day in a temperature of 96° or 98° in the shade, running up sometimes to 103° at midnight. Very few men, even though they get a pannikin of flat, stale, muddy beer and hide it under their cots, can continue drinking for six hours a day. One man tried, but he died, and nearly the whole regiment went to his funeral because it gave them something to do. It was too early for the modified excitement of fever or cholera. The men could only wait and wait and wait, and watch the shadow of the barrack creeping across the blinding white dust. That was a gay life !

They lounged about cantonments—it was too hot for any sort of game, and almost too hot for vice—and fuddled themselves in the evening, and filled themselves to distention with the healthy nitrogenous food provided for them, and the more they stoked the less exercise they took and more explosive they grew. Then the tempers began to wear away, and men fell a-brooding over insults real or imaginary. They had nothing else to think of. The tone of the " repartees " changed, and instead of saying light-heartedly : " I'll knock your silly face in," men grew laboriously polite and hinted that the cantonments were not big enough for themselves and their enemy, and that there would be more space for one of the two in a Place which it is not polite to mention.

It may have been the Devil who arranged the thing, but the fact of the case is that Losson had for a long time been worrying Simmons in an aimless way. It gave him occupation. The two men had their cots side by side, and would sometimes spend a long afternoon swearing at each other ; but Simmons was afraid of Losson and dared not challenge him to a fight. He thought over the words in the hot still nights, and half the hate he felt towards Losson he vented on the wretched punkah-coolie.

Losson bought a parrot in the bazar, and put it into a

little cage, and lowered the cage into the cool darkness of a well, and sat on the well-kerb, shouting bad language down to the parrot. He taught it to say : "Simmons, ye *so-oor,*" which means swine, and several other things entirely unfit for publication. He was a big gross man, and he shook like a jelly when the parrot caught the sentence correctly. Simmons, however, shook with rage, for all the room were laughing at him—the parrot was such a disreputable puff of green feathers and looked so human when it chattered. Losson used to sit, swinging his fat legs, on the side of the cot, and ask the parrot what it thought of Simmons. The parrot would answer :—" Simmons, ye *so-oor* ". " Good boy," Losson used to say, scratching the parrot's head ; " ye 'ear that, Sim ? " And Simmons used to turn over on his stomach and make answer : " I 'ear. Take 'eed *you* don't 'ear something one of these days ".

In the restless nights, after he had been asleep all day, fits of blind rage came upon Simmons and held him till he trembled all over, while he thought in how many different ways he would slay Losson. Sometimes he would picture himself trampling the life out of the man, with heavy ammunition boots, and at others smashing in his face with the butt, and at others jumping on his shoulders and dragging the head back till the neck-bone cracked. Then his mouth would feel hot and fevered, and he would reach out for another sup of the beer in the pannikin.

But the fancy that came to him most frequently and stayed with him longest was one connected with the great roll of fat under Losson's right ear. He noticed it first on a moonlight night, and thereafter it was always before his eyes. It was a fascinating roll of fat. A man could get his hand upon it and tear away one side of the neck ; or he could place the muzzle of a rifle on it and blow away all the head in a flash. Losson had no right to be sleek and contented and well-to-do, when he, Simmons, was the butt of the room. Some day, perhaps, he would show those who laughed at the " Simmons, ye *so-oor* " joke, that he was as good as the rest,

and held a man's life in the crook of his forefinger. When
Losson snored, Simmons hated him more bitterly than ever.
Why should Losson be able to sleep when Simmons had to stay
awake hour after hour, tossing and turning on the tapes, with
the dull pain gnawing into his right side and his head throbbing
and aching after Canteen? He thought over this for many
many nights, and the world became unprofitable to him. He
even blunted his naturally fine appetite with beer and tobacco;
and all the while the parrot talked at and made a mock of him.

The heat continued and the tempers wore away more
quickly than before. A Sergeant's wife died of heat-apoplexy
in the night, and the rumour ran abroad that it was cholera.
Men rejoiced openly, hoping that it would spread and send
them into camp. But that was a false alarm.

It was late on a Tuesday evening, and the men were
waiting in the deep double verandahs for " Last Posts," when
Simmons went to the box at the foot of his bed, took out
his pipe, and slammed the lid down with a bang that echoed
through the deserted barrack like the crack of a rifle.
Ordinarily speaking, the men would have taken no notice;
but their nerves were fretted to fiddle-strings. They jumped
up, and three or four clattered into the barrack-room only to
find Simmons kneeling by his box.

" Ow! It's you, is it?" they said and laughed foolishly;
" we thought 't was——"

Simmons rose slowly. If the accident had so shaken his
fellows, what would not the reality do?

"You thought it was—did you? And what makes you
think?" he said, lashing himself into madness as he went
on; "to Hell with your thinking, ye dirty spies."

" Simmons, ye *so-oor*," chuckled the parrot in the verandah
sleepily, recognizing a well known voice. And that was
absolutely all.

The tension snapped. Simmons fell back on the arm-
rack deliberately, the men were at the far end of the room,
and took out his rifle and packet of ammunition. " Don't go

playing the goat, Sim!" said Losson; "put it down," but there was a quaver in his voice. Another man stooped, slipped his boot and hurled it at Simmons' head. The prompt answer was a shot which, fired at random, found its billet in Losson's throat. Losson fell forward without a word, and the others scattered.

"You thought it was!" yelled Simmons. "You're drivin' me to it! I tell you you're drivin' me to it! Get up, Losson, an' don't lie shammin' there—you an' your blasted parrit that druv me to it!"

But there was an unaffected reality about Losson's pose that showed Simmons what he had done. The men were still clamouring in the verandah. Simmons appropriated two more packets of ammunition and ran into the moonlight, muttering: "I'll make a night of it. Thirty roun's, an' the last for myself. Take you that, you dogs!"

He dropped on one knee and fired into the brown of the men in the verandah, but the bullet flew high, and landed in the brick-work with a vicious *phwit* that made some of the younger men turn pale. It is, as musketry theorists observe, one thing to fire and another to be fired at.

Then the instinct of the chase flared up. The news spread from barrack to barrack, and the men doubled out intent on the capture of Simmons, the wild beast, who was heading for the Cavalry parade-ground, stopping now and again to send back a shot and a curse in the direction of his pursuers.

"I'll learn you to spy on me!" he shouted; "I'll learn you to give me dorg's names! Come on the 'ole lot o' you! Colonel John Anthony Deever, C.B.!"——he turned towards the Infantry Mess and shook his rifle——"You think yourself the devil of a man—but I tell you that if you put your ugly old carcase outside o' that door, I'll make you the poorest lookin' man in the army. Come out, Colonel John Anthony Deever, C.B.! Come out and see me practiss on the rainge. I'm the crack shot of the 'ole bloomin' battalion." In proof of which statement Simmons fired at the lighted windows of the mess-house.

"Private Simmons, E Comp'ny, on the Cavalry p'rade-ground, Sir, with thirty rounds," said a Sergeant breathlessly to the Colonel. "Shootin' right and lef', Sir. Shot Private Losson. What's to be done, Sir?"

Colonel John Anthony Deever, C.B., sallied out, only to be saluted by a spirt of dust at his feet.

"Pull up!" said the Second in Command; "I don't want my step in that way, Colonel. He's as dangerous as a mad dog."

"Shoot him like one, then," said the Colonel bitterly, "if he won't take his chance. *My* regiment, too! If it had been the Towheads I could have understood."

Private Simmons had occupied a strong position near a well on the edge of the parade-ground, and was defying the regiment to come on. The regiment was not anxious to comply with the request, for there is small honour in being shot by a fellow-private. Only Corporal Slane, rifle in hand, threw himself down on the ground and wormed his way towards the well.

"Don't shoot," said he to the men round him; "like as not you'll 'it me. I'll catch the beggar, livin'."

Simmons ceased shouting for a while, and the noise of trap-wheels could be heard across the plain. Major Oldyne, Commanding the Horse Battery, was coming back from a dinner in the Civil Lines; was driving after his usual custom—that is to say, as fast as the horse could go.

"A orf'cer! A blooming spangled orf'cer!" shrieked Simmons; "I'll make a scarecrow of that orf'cer!" The trap stopped.

"What's this?" demanded the Major of Gunners. "You there, drop your rifle."

"Why, it's Jerry Blazes! I ain't got no quarrel with you, Jerry Blazes. Pass frien', an' all's well!"

But Jerry Blazes had not the faintest intention of passing a dangerous murderer. He was, as his adoring Battery swore long and fervently, without knowledge of fear, and they were surely the best judges, for Jerry Blazes, it was notorious, had

done his possible to kill a man each time the Battery
went out.

He walked towards Simmons, with the intention of
rushing him and knocking him down.

"Don't make me do it, Sir," said Simmons; "I ain't got
nothing agin you. Ah! you would?"——the Major broke
into a run—"Take that then!"

The Major dropped with a bullet through his shoulder,
and Simmons stood over him. He had lost the satisfaction
of killing Losson in the desired way: but here was a helpless
body to his hand. Should he slip in another cartridge and
blow off the head, or with the butt smash in the white face?
He stopped to consider, and a cry went up from the far side
of the parade-ground:—"He's killed Jerry Blazes!" But in
the shelter of the well-pillars Simmons was safe, except when
he stepped out to fire. "I'll blow yer 'andsome 'ead off,
Jerry Blazes," said Simmons reflectively; "six an' three is
nine an' one is ten, an' that leaves me another nineteen, an'
one for myself." He tugged at the string of the second
packet of ammunition. Corporal Slane crawled out of the
shadow of a bank into the moonlight.

"I see you!" said Simmons; "come a bit furder on an'
I'll do for you."

"I'm comin'," said Corporal Slane briefly; "you done a
bad day's work, Sim. Come out 'ere an' come back with me."

"Come to ——," laughed Simmons, sending a cartridge
home with his thumb. "Not before I've settled you an' Jerry
Blazes."

The Corporal was lying at full length in the dust of the
parade-ground, a rifle under him. Some of the less cautious
men in the distance shouted:—"Shoot 'im! Shoot 'im,
Slane!"

"You move 'and or foot, Slane," said Simmons, "an' I'll
kick Jerry Blazes' 'ead in, and shoot you after."

"I ain't movin'," said the Corporal, raising his head;
"you daren't 'it a man on 'is legs. Let go o' Jerry Blazes

an' come out o' that with your fistes. Come an' 'it me. You daren't, you bloomin' dog-shooter ! "

" I dare."

" You lie, you man-sticker. You sneakin', sheeny butcher, you lie. See there ! " Slane kicked the rifle away and stood up in the peril of his life. " Come on now ! "

The temptation was more than Simmons could resist, for the Corporal in his white clothes offered a perfect mark.

" Don't misname me," shouted Simmons, firing as he spoke. The shot missed, and the shooter, blind with rage, threw his rifle down and rushed at Slane from the protection of the well. Within striking distance, he kicked savagely at Slane's stomach, but the weedy Corporal knew something of Simmons' weakness, and knew, too, the deadly guard for that kick. Bowing forward and drawing up his right leg till the heel of the right foot was set some three inches above the inside of the left knee-cap, he met the blow standing on one leg— exactly as Gonds stand when they meditate—and ready for the fall that would follow. There was an oath, the Corporal fell over to his own left as shinbone met shinbone, and the Private collapsed, his right leg broken an inch above the ankle.

" Pity you don't know that guard, Sim," said Slane, spitting out the dust as he rose. Then raising his voice— " Come an' take him orf. I've bruk 'is leg". This was not strictly true, for the Private had accomplished his own downfall, since it is the special merit of that leg-guard that the harder the kick the greater the kicker's discomfiture.

Slane walked to Jerry Blazes and hung over him with exaggerated solicitude, while Simmons, weeping with pain, was carried away. " 'Ope you ain't 'urt badly, Sir," said Slane. The Major had fainted, and there was an ugly ragged hole through the top of his arm. Slane knelt down and murmured :—" S'elp me, I believe 'e's dead. Well, if that ain't my blooming luck all over ! "

But the Major was destined to lead his Battery afield for many a long day with unshaken nerve. He was removed, and nursed and petted into convalescence, while the Battery discussed the wisdom of capturing Simmons and blowing him from a gun. They idolized their Major, and his re-appearance on parade resulted in a scene nowhere provided for in the Army Regulations.

Great, too, was the glory that fell to Slane's share. The Gunners would have made him drunk thrice a day for at least a fortnight. Even the Colonel of his own regiment complimented him upon his coolness, and the local paper called him a hero. Which things did not puff him up. When the Major proffered him money and thanks, the virtuous Corporal took the one and put aside the other. But he had a request to make and prefaced it with many a "Beg y' pardon, Sir". Could the Major see his way to letting the Slane-McKenna wedding be adorned by the presence of four Battery horses to pull a hired barouche? The Major could, and so could the Battery. Excessively so. It was a gorgeous wedding.

*　　　*　　　*　　　*　　　*　　　*　　　*

"Wot did I do it for?" said Corporal Slane. "For the 'orses o' course. Jhansi ain't a beauty to look at, but I wasn't goin' to 'ave a hired turn-out. Jerry Blazes? If I 'adn't a wanted something, Sim might ha' blowed Jerry Blazes' blooming 'ead into Hirish stew for aught I'd 'a cared.'

And they hanged Private Simmons—hanged him as high as Haman in hollow square of the regiment; and the Colonel said it was Drink; and the Chaplain was sure it was the Devil; and Simmons fancied it was both, but he didn't know, and only hoped his fate would be a warning to his companions; and half-a-dozen "intelligent publicists" wrote six beautiful leading articles on "The Prevalence of Crime in the Army".

But not a soul thought of comparing the "bloody-minded Simmons" to the squawking, gaping school-girl with which this story opens.

That would have been too absurd!

DANNY DEEVER

'WHAT are the bugles blowin' for?' said Files-on-
  Parade.
'To turn you out, to turn you out,' the Colour-
  Sergeant said.
'What makes you look so white, so white?' said
  Files-on-Parade.
'I'm dreadin' what I've got to watch,' the Colour-
  Sergeant said.
  For they're hangin' Danny Deever, you can
    hear the Dead March play,
  The regiment's in 'ollow square—they're
    hangin' him to-day;
  They've taken of his buttons off an' cut his
    stripes away,
  An' they're hangin' Danny Deever in the
    mornin'.

3

'What makes the rear-rank breathe so 'ard?' said
    Files-on-Parade.
'It's bitter cold, it's bitter cold,' the Colour-
    Sergeant said.
'What makes that front-rank man fall down?' says
    Files-on-Parade.
'A touch o' sun, a touch o' sun,' the Colour-Sergeant
    said.

    They are hangin' Danny Deever, they are
        marchin' of 'im round,
    They 'ave 'alted Danny Deever by 'is coffin
        on the ground;
    An' 'e'll swing in 'arf a minute for a sneakin'
        shootin' hound—
    O they're hangin' Danny Deever in the
        mornin'!

''Is cot was right-'and cot to mine,' said Files-on-
    Parade.
''E's sleepin' out an' far to-night,' the Colour-
    Sergeant said.
'I've drunk 'is beer a score o' times,' said Files-on-
    Parade.
''E's drinkin' bitter beer alone,' the Colour-Sergeant
    said.

They are hangin' Danny Deever, you must mark 'im to 'is place,

For 'e shot a comrade sleepin'—you must look 'im in the face;

Nine 'undred of 'is county an' the regiment's disgrace,

While they're hangin' Danny Deever in the mornin'.

'What's that so black agin the sun?' said Files-on-Parade.

'It's Danny fightin' 'ard for life,' the Colour-Sergeant said.

'What's that that whimpers over'ead?' said Files-on-Parade.

'It's Danny's soul that's passin' now,' the Colour-Sergeant said.

For they're done with Danny Deever, you can 'ear the quickstep play,

The regiment's in column, an' they're marchin' us away;

Ho! the young recruits are shakin', an' they'll want their beer to-day,

After hangin' Danny Deever in the mornin'.

BLACK JACK.

To the wake av Tim O'Hara
Came company,
All St. Patrick's Alley
Was there to see.
—*The Wake of Tim O'Hara.*

THERE is a writer called Mr. Robert Louis Stevenson, who makes most delicate inlay-work in black and white, and files out to the fraction of a hair. He has written a story about a Suicide Club, wherein men gambled for Death because other amusements did not bite sufficiently. My friend Private Mulvaney knows nothing about Mr. Stevenson, but he once assisted informally at a meeting of almost such a club as that gentleman has described; and his words are true.

As the Three Musketeers share their silver, tobacco, and liquor together, as they protect each other in barracks or camp, and as they rejoice together over the joy of one, so do they divide their sorrows. When Ortheris' irrepressible tongue has brought him into cells for a season, or Learoyd has run amok through his kit and accoutrements, or Mulvaney has indulged in strong waters, and under their influence reproved his Commanding Officer, you can see the trouble in the faces of the untouched twain. And the rest of the regiment know that comment or jest is unsafe. Generally the three avoid Orderly Room and the Corner Shop that follows, leaving both to the young bloods who have not sown their wild oats ; but there are occasions . . .

For instance, Ortheris was sitting on the drawbridge of the main gate of Fort Amara, with his hands in his pockets and his pipe, bowl down, in his mouth. Learoyd was lying at full length on the turf of the glacis, kicking his heels in the air, and I came round the corner and asked for Mulvaney.

Ortheris spat into the ditch and shook his head. " No good seein' 'im now," said Ortheris ; " 'e's a bloomin' camel. Listen ! "

I heard on the flags of the verandah opposite to the cells, which are close to the Guard Room, a measured step that I could have identified in the tramp of an army. There were twenty paces *crescendo*, a pause, and then twenty *diminuendo*.

" That's 'im," said Ortheris ; " my Gawd, that's 'im ! All for a bloomin' button you could see your face in an' a bit o' lip that a bloomin' Harkangel would 'a guv back."

Mulvaney was doing pack-drill—was compelled, that is to say, to walk up and down for certain hours in full marching order, with rifle, bayonet, ammunition, knapsack, and overcoat. And his offence was being dirty on parade ! I nearly fell into the Fort Ditch with astonishment and wrath, for Mulvaney is the smartest man that ever mounted guard, and would as soon think of turning out uncleanly as of dispensing with his trousers.

" Who was the Sergeant that checked him ? " I asked.

" Mullins, o' course," said Ortheris.   " There ain't no other man would whip 'im on the peg so.   But Mullins ain't a man. 'E's a dirty, little pigscraper, that's wot 'e is."

" What did Mulvaney say ?   He's not the make of man to take that quietly."

" Said !   Bin better for 'im if 'e'd shut 'is mouth.   Lord, 'ow we laughed !   ' Sargint,' 'e sez, ' ye say I'm dirty.   Well,' sez 'e, ' when your wife lets you blow your own nose for yourself, perhaps you'll know wot dirt is.   You're him-perfectly eddicated, Sargint,' sez 'e, an' then we fell in. But after p'rade, 'e was up an' Mullins was swearin' 'imself black in the face at Ord'ly Room that Mulvaney 'ad called 'im a swine an' Lord knows wot all.   You know Mullins. 'E'll 'ave 'is 'ead broke in one o' these days.   'E's too big a bloomin' liar for ord'nary consumption.   ' Three hours' can an' kit,' sez the Colonel ; ' not for bein' dirty on p'rade, but for 'avin' said somethin' to Mullins, tho' I do not believe,' sez 'e, ' you said wot 'e said you said.' An' Mulvaney fell away sayin' nothin'. You know 'e never speaks to the Colonel for fear o' gettin' 'imself fresh copped."

Mullins, a very young and very much married Sergeant, whose manners were partly the result of innate depravity and partly of imperfectly digested Board School, came over the bridge, and most rudely asked Ortheris what he was doing.

"Me?" said Ortheris. "'Ow! I'm waiting for my C'mission. 'Seed it comin' along yit?"

Mullins turned purple and passed on. There was the sound of a gentle chuckle from the glacis where Learoyd lay.

"'E expects to get his C'mission some day," explained Orth'ris; "Gawd 'elp the Mess that 'ave to put their 'ands into the same kiddy as 'im! Wot time d'you make it, Sir? Fower! Mulvaney 'll be out in 'arf an hour. You don't want to buy a dorg, Sir, do you? A pup you can trust—'arf Rampore by the Colonel's grey 'ound."

"Ortheris," I answered sternly, for I knew what was in his mind, "do you mean to say that—— "

"I didn't mean to arx money o' you, any'ow," said Ortheris; "I'd 'a sold you the dorg good an' cheap but—but —I know Mulvaney 'll want somethin' after we've walked 'im orf, an' I ain't got nothin', nor 'e 'asn't neither. I'd sooner sell you the dorg, Sir. 'S trewth I would!"

A shadow fell on the drawbridge, and Ortheris began to rise into the air, lifted by a huge hand upon his collar.

"Onything but t' braass," said Learoyd, quietly, as he held the Londoner over the ditch. "Onything but t' braass, Orth'ris, ma son! Ah 've got one rupee eight annas of ma own.' He showed two coins, and replaced Ortheris on the drawbridge rail.

"Very good," I said; "where are you going to?"

"Goin' to walk 'im orf when 'e comes out—two miles or three or fower," said Ortheris.

The footsteps within ceased. I heard the dull thud of a knapsack falling on a bedstead, followed by the rattle of arms. Ten minutes later, Mulvaney, faultlessly attired, his lips compressed and his face as black as a thunderstorm, stalked into the sunshine on the drawbridge. Learoyd and Ortheris sprang from my side and closed in upon him, both leaning towards as horses lean upon the pole. In an instant they had disappeared down the sunken road to the cantonments, and I was left alone. Mulvaney had not seen fit to recognize me; wherefore, I felt that his trouble must be heavy upon him.

I climbed one of the bastions and watched the figures of the Three Musketeers grow smaller and smaller across the plain. They were walking as fast as they could put foot to the ground, and their heads were bowed. They fetched a great compass round the parade-ground, skirted the Cavalry lines, and vanished in the belt of trees that fringes the low land by the river.

I followed slowly, and sighted them—dusty, sweating, but still keeping up their long, swinging tramp—on the river bank. They crashed through the Forest Reserve, headed towards the Bridge of Boats, and presently established themselves on the bow of one of the pontoons. I rode cautiously till I saw three puffs of white smoke rise and die out in the clear evening air, and knew that peace had come again. At the bridge-head they waved me forward with gestures of welcome.

"Tie up your 'orse," shouted Ortheris, "an' come on, sir. We're all goin' 'ome in this 'ere bloomin' boat."

From the bridge-head to the Forest Officer's bungalow is but a step. The mess-man was there, and would see that a man held my horse. Did the Sahib require aught else—a peg, or beer? Ritchie Sahib had left half-a-dozen bottles of the latter, but since the Sahib was a friend of Ritchie Sahib and he, the mess-man, was a poor man——

I gave my order quietly, and returned to the bridge. Mulvaney had taken off his boots, and was dabbling his toes in the water; Learoyd was lying on his back on the pontoon; and Ortheris was pretending to row with a big bamboo.

" I'm an ould fool," said Mulvaney, reflectively, " dhraggin' you two out here bekase I **was** undher the Black Dog—sulkin' like a child. Me that was soldierin' when Mullins, an' be damned to him, was shqualin' on a counterpin for foive shillin's a week, an' that not paid! Bhoys, I've took you foive miles out av natural pevarsity. Phew!"

" Wot's the odds as long as you're 'appy?" said Ortheris applying himself afresh to the bamboo. " As well 'ere as anywhere else."

Learoyd held up a rupee and an eight-anna bit, and shook his head sorrowfully. " Five mile from t' Canteen, all along o' Mulvaney's blaasted pride."

" I know ut," said Mulvaney, penitently. " Why will ye come wid me? An' yet I wud be mortial sorry if ye did not —any time—though I am ould enough to know betther. But I will do penance. I will take a dhrink av wather."

Ortheris squeaked shrilly. The butler of the Forest bungalow was standing near the railings with a basket, uncertain how to clamber down to the pontoon.

" Might a know'd you'd a got liquor out o' a bloomin' desert, sir," said Ortheris, gracefully, to me. Then, to the mess-man: " Easy with them there bottles. They're worth their weight in gold. Jock, ye long-armed beggar, get out o' that an' hike 'em down."

Learoyd had the basket on the pontoon in an instant, and the Three Musketeers gathered round it with dry lips. They drank my health in due and ancient form, and thereafter tobacco tasted sweeter than ever. They absorbed all the beer, and disposed themselves in picturesque attitudes to admire the setting sun,—no man speaking for a while.

Mulvaney's head dropped upon his chest, and we thought that he was asleep.

" What on earth did you come so far for?" I whispered to Ortheris.

" To walk 'im orf, o' course. When 'e's been checked we allus walks 'im orf. 'E ain't fit to be spoke to those times—

nor 'e ain't fit to leave alone neither. So we takes 'im till
'e is."

Mulvaney raised his head, and stared straight into the
sunset. " I had my rifle," said he, dreamily, " an' I had my
baynit, an' Mullins came round the corner, an' he looked in
my face an' grinned dishpiteful. ' *You* can't blow your own
nose,' sez he. Now, I cannot tell fwhat Mullins' expayrience
may ha' been, but, Mother av God, he was nearer to his death
that minut' than I have iver been to mine—and that's less
than the thicknuss av a hair ! "

" Yes," said Ortheris, calmly, " you'd look fine with all
your buttons took orf, an' the Band in front o' you, walkin'
roun' slow time. We're both front-rank men, me an' Jock,
when the rig'ment's in 'ollow square. Bloomin' fine you'd
look. ' The Lord giveth an' the Lord taketh awai—Heasy
with that there drop !—Blessed be the naime o' the Lord.' "
He gulped in a quaint and suggestive fashion.

" Mullins ! Wot's Mullins ? " said Learoyd, slowly.
" Ah'd take a coomp'ny o' Mullinses—ma hand behind
me. Sitha, Mulvaney, dunnot be a fool."

" *You* were not checked for fwhat you did not do, an'
made a mock av afther. 'Twas for less than that the Tyrone
wud ha' sent O'Hara to hell, instid av lettin' him go by his
own choosin', whin Rafferty shot him," retorted Mulvaney.

" And who stopped the Tyrone from doing it ? " I asked.

" That ould fool who's sorry he didn't shtick the pig
Mullins." His head dropped again. When he raised it he
shivered and put his hands on the shoulders of his two
companions.

" Ye've walked the Divil out av me, bhoys," said he.

Ortheris shot out the red-hot dottel of his pipe on the
back of the hairy fist. " They say 'Ell's 'otter than that,"
said he, as Mulvaney swore aloud. " You be warned so.
Look yonder !"—he pointed across the river to a ruined
temple—" Me an' you an' '*im* "—he indicated me by a jerk
of his head—" was there one day when Hi made a bloomin'

show o' myself. You an' 'im stopped me doin' such—an' Hi
was on'y wishful for to desert. You are makin' a bigger
bloomin' show o' yourself now."

"Don't mind him, Mulvaney," I said ; " Dinah Shadd
won't let you hang yourself yet awhile, and you don't intend
to try it either. Let's hear about the Tyrone and O'Hara.
Rafferty shot him for fooling with his wife. What happened
before that ?"

"There's no fool like an ould fool. You know you can
do anythin' wid me whin I'm talkin'. Did I say I wud like
to cut Mullins' liver out ? I deny the imputashin, for fear
that Orth'ris here wud report me—Ah ! You wud tip me
into the river, wud you ? Sit quiet, little man. Anyways,
Mullins is not worth the trouble av an extry p'rade, an' I
will trate him wid outrajis contimpt. The Tyrone an'
O'Hara ! O'Hara an' the Tyrone, begad ! Ould days are
hard to bring back into the mouth, but they're always inside
the head."

Followed a long pause.

" O'Hara was a Divil. Though I saved him, for the
honour av the rig'mint, from his death that time, I say it
now. He was a Divil—a long, bould, black-haired Divil."

" Which way ?" asked Ortheris.

"Women."

" Then I know another."

" Not more than in reason, if you mane me, ye warped
walkin-shtick. I have been young, an' for why should I not
have tuk what I cud ? Did I iver, whin I was Corp'ril, use
the rise av my rank—wan step an' that taken away, more's
the sorrow an' the fault av me !—to prosecute a nefarious
inthrigue, as O'Hara did ? Did I, whin I was Corp'ril, lay
my spite upon a man an' make his life a dog's life from day
to day ? Did I lie, as O'Hara lied, till the young wans in the
Tyrone turned white wid the fear av the Judgment av God
killin' thim all in a lump, as ut killed the woman at Devizes ?
I did not ! I have sinned my sins an' I have made my con-

6

fesshin, an' Father Victor knows the worst av me.　O'Hara
was tuk, before he cud spake, on Rafferty's door-step, an' no
man knows the worst av him.　But this much I know !

"The Tyrone was recruited any fashion in the ould days,
A draf' from Connemara—a draf' from Portsmouth— a draf'
from Kerry, an' that was a blazin' bad draf'—here there and
ivrywhere—but the large av thim was Oirish—Black Oirish.
Now there are Oirish an' Oirish.　The good are 'good as the
best, but the bad are wurrst than the wurrst.　'Tis this way.
They clog together in pieces as fast as thieves, an' no wan
knows fwhat they will do till wan turns informer an' the
gang is bruk.　But ut begins again, a day later, meetin' in
holes an' corners an' swearin' bloody oaths an' shtickin' a
man in the back an' runnin' away, an' thin waitin' for the
blood-money on the reward papers—to see if ut's worth
enough.　Those are the Black Oirish an' 'tis they that bring
dishgrace upon the name av Oireland, an' thim I wud kill—
as I nearly killed wan wanst.

"But to reshume.　My room—'twas before I was married
—was wid twelve av the scum av the earth—the pickin's av
the gutter—mane men that wud neither laugh nor talk nor
yet get dhrunk as a man shud.　They thried some av their
dog's thricks on me, but I dhrew a line round my cot, an' the
man that thransgressed ut wint into hospital for three days
good.

"O'Hara had put his spite on the room—he was my Colour
Sargint—an' nothin' cud we do to plaze him.　I was younger
than I am now, an' I tuk what I got in the way av dressing
down and punishmint-dhrill wid my tongue in my cheek.
But it was diff'rint wid the others, an' why I cannot say, excipt
that some men are borrun mane an' go to dhirty murdher
where a fist is more than enough.　Afther a whoile, they
changed their chune to me an' was des'prit frien'ly—all
twelve av thim cursin' O'Hara in chorus.

"'Eyah,' sez I, 'O'Hara's a divil and I'm not for denyin'
ut, but is he the only man in the wurruld?　Let him go

He'll get tired av findin' our kit foul an' our 'coutrements onproperly kep.'

" ' We will *not* let him go,' sez they.

" ' Thin take him,' sez I, 'an' a dashed poor yield you will get for your throuble.'

" ' Is he not misconductin' himself wid Slimmy's wife ? ' sez another.

" ' She's common to the rig'mint,' sez I. 'Fwhat has made ye this partic'lar on a suddint ? '

" ' Has he not put his spite on the roomful av us ? Can we do anythin' that he will not check us for ? ' sez another.

" ' That's thrue,' sez I.

" ' Will ye not help us to do aught,' sez another—'a big bould man like you ? '

" ' I will break his head upon his shoulthers av he puts hand on me,' sez I. ' I will give him the lie av he says that I'm dhirty, an' I wud not mind duckin' him in the Artillery troughs if ut was not that I'm thryin' for my shtripes.'

" ' Is that all ye will do ? ' sez another. ' Have ye no more spunk than that, ye blood-dhrawn calf ? '

" ' Blood-dhrawn I may be,' sez I, gettin' back to my cot an' makin' my line round ut; 'but ye know that the man who comes acrost this mark will be more blood-dhrawn than me. No man gives me the name in my mouth,' I sez ' Ondersthand, I will have no part wid you in anythin' ye do, nor will I raise my fist to my shuperior. Is any wan comin' on ? ' sez I.

" They made no move, tho' I gave thim full time, but stud growlin' an' snarlin' together at wan ind av the room. I tuk up my cap and wint out to Canteen, thinkin' no little av mesilf, an' there I grew most ondacintly dhrunk in my legs. My head was all reasonable.

" ' Houligan,' I sez to a man in E Comp'ny that was by way av bein' a frind av mine; 'I'm overtuk from the belt down. Do you give me the touch av your shoulther to presarve my formation an' march me acrost the ground into the high grass. I'll sleep ut off there,' sez I; an' Houligan—he's dead now, but good he was while he lasted—walked wid me, givin' me the touch whin I wint wide, ontil we came to the high grass, an', my faith, the sky an' the earth was fair rowlin' undher me. I made for where the grass was thickust, an' there I slep' off my liquor wid an easy conscience. I did not desire to come on books too frequint; my characther havin' been shpotless for the good half av a year.

"Whin I roused, the dhrink was dyin' out in me an' I felt as tho' a she-cat had littered in my mouth. I had not learned to hould my liquor wid comfort in thim days. 'Tis little betther I am now. 'I will get Houligan to pour a bucket over my head,' thinks I, an' I wud ha' risen, but I heard some wan say :—' Mulvaney can take the blame av ut for the backslidin' hound he is'.

"'Oho !' sez I, an' my head rang like a guard-room gong ; 'fwhat is the blame that this young man must take to oblige Tim Vulmea ?' For 'twas Tim Vulmea that shpoke.

"I turned on my belly an' crawled through the grass, a bit at a time, to where the spache came from. There was the twelve av my room sittin' down in a little patch, the dhry grass wavin' above their heads an' the sin av black murdher in their hearts. I put the stuff aside to get clear view.

"' Fwhat's that ? ' sez wan man, jumpin' up.

"' A dog, sez Vulmea. ' You're a nice hand to this job ! As I said, Mulvaney will take the blame—av ut comes to a pinch.'

"' 'Tis harrd to swear a man's life away,' sez a young wan.

"' Thank ye for that,' thinks I. 'Now, fwhat the divil are you paragins conthrivin' against me ?'

"' 'Tis as easy as dhrinkin' your quart,' sez Vulmea. ' At seven or thereon O'Hara will come acrost to the Married Quarters, goin' to call on Slimmy's wife, the swine ! Wan av us'll pass the wurrd to the room an' we shtart the divil an' all av a shine—laughin' an' crackin' on an' t'rowin' our boots about. Thin O'Hara will come to give us the ordher to be quiet, the more by token bekaze the room-lamp will be knocked over in the larkin'. He will take the straight road to the ind door where there's the lamp in the verandah, an' that'll bring him clear against the light as he shtands. He will not be able to look into the dhark. Wan av us will loose off, an' a close shot ut will be, an' shame to the man that misses. Twill be Mulvaney's rifle, she that is at the head av the rack —there's no mistakin' that long-shtocked, cross-eyed bitch even in the dhark.'

"The thief misnamed my ould firin' piece out av jealousy— I was pershuaded av that—an' ut made me more angry than all.

"But Vulmea goes on :—' O'Hara will dhrop, an' by the time the light's lit again, there'll be some six av us on the chest av Mulvaney, cryin' murdher an' rape. Mulvaney's cot is near the ind door, an' the shmokin' rifle will be lyin' undher him whin we've knocked him over. We know, an' all the rig'mint knows, that Mulvaney has given O'Hara more lip than any man av us. Will there be any doubt at the Coort-Martial? Wud twelve honust sodger-bhoys swear away the life av a dear, quiet, swate-timpered man such as is Mulvaney—wid his line av pipe-clay roun' his cot, threat- enin' us wid murdher av we overshtepped ut, as we can truthful testify?'

"'Mary, Mother av Mercy!' thinks I to mesilf; 'it is this to have an unruly mimber an' fistes fit to use! O the sneakin' hounds!'

"The big dhrops ran down my face, for I was wake wid the liquor an' had not the full av my wits about me. I laid shtill an' heard thim workin' themselves up to swear my life by tellin' tales av ivry time I had put my mark on wan or another; an', my faith, they was few that was not so dish- tinguished. 'Twas all in the way av fair fight, though, for niver did I raise my hand excipt whin they had provoked me to ut.

" ' 'Tis all well,' sez wan av thim, ' but who's to do this shootin ' ? '

" ' Fwhat matther ? ' sez Vulmea.   ' 'Tis Mulvaney will do that—at the Coort-Martial.'

" ' He will so,' sez the man, ' but who's hand is put to the thrigger—*in the room ?* '

" ' Who'll do ut ? ' sez Vulmea lookin' round, but divil a man answeared.   They began to dishpute till Kiss, that was always playin' Shpoil Five, sez :—' Thry the kyards ! ' Wid that he opined his jackut an' tuk out the greasy palammers, an' they all fell in wid the notion.

" ' Deal on ! ' sez Vulmea, wid a big rattlin' oath, ' an' the Black Curse av Shielygh come to the man that will not do his duty as the kyards say.   Amin ! '

" ' Black Jack is the masther,' sez Kiss, dealin'.   Black Jack, Sorr, I shud expaytiate to you, is the Ace av Shpades which from time immimorial has been intimately connect wid battle, murdher an' suddin death.

" *Wanst* Kiss dealt an' there was no sign, but the men was whoite wid the workin's av their sowls.   *Twice* Kiss dealt, an' there was a grey shine on their cheeks like the mess av an egg.   *Three* times Kiss dealt an' they was blue ; ' Have ye not lost him ? ' sez Vulmea, wiping the sweat on him ; ' Let's ha' done quick ? '   ' Quick ut is,' sez Kiss t'rowin' him the kyard ; an' ut fell face up on his knee—Black Jack !

" Thin they all cackled wid laughin.'   ' Duty thrippence,' sez one av thim, ' an' damned cheap at that price ! '   But I cud see they all dhrew a little away from Vulmea an' lef' him sittin' playin' wid the kyard.   Vulmea sez no word for a whoile but licked his lips—cat-ways.   Thin he threw up his head an' made the men swear by ivry oath known an' unknown to stand by him not alone in the room but at the Coort-Martial that was to set on me !   He tould off five av the biggest to stretch me on my cot whin the shot was fired, an' another man he tould off to put out the light, an' yet an-

other to load my rifle. He wud not do that himself· an' that
was quare, for 't was but a little thing.

"Thin they swore over again that they wud not bethray
wan another, an' crep' out av the grass in diff'rint ways,
two by two. A mercy ut was that they did not come on me.
I was sick wid fear in the pit av my stummick—sick, sick,
sick! Afther they was all gone, I wint back to Canteen an
called for a quart to put a thought in me. Vulmea was there,
dhrinkin' heavy, an' politeful to me beyond reason. 'Fwhat
will I do—fwhat will I do?' thinks I to mesilf whin Vulmea
wint away.

" Presintly the Arm'rer Sargint comes in stiffin' an crackin
on, not pleased wid any wan, bekaze the Martini Henri bein'
new to the rig'mint in those days we used to play the mischief
wid her arrangemints. 'Twas a long time before I cud get
out av the way av thryin' to pull back the back-sight an'
turnin' her over afther firin'—as if she was a Snider.

"'Fwhat tailor-men do they give me to work wid?' sez
the Arm'rer Sargint. 'Here's Hogan, his nose flat as a table,
laid by for a week, an' ivry Comp'ny sendin' their arrums in
knocked to small shivreens.'

"'Fwhat's wrong wid Hogan, Sargint?' sez I.

"'Wrong!' sez the Arm'rer Sargint; 'I showed him, as
though I had been his mother, the way av shtrippin a 'Tini,
an' he shtrup her clane an' easy. I tould him to put her to
again an' fire a blank into the blow-pit to show how the dirt
hung on the groovin'. He did that, but he did not put in the
pin av the fallin'-block, an' av coorse whin he fired he was
strook by the block jumpin' clear. Well for him 'twas but
a blank—a full charge wud ha' cut his oi out.'

" I looked a trifle wiser than a boiled sheep's head. 'How's
that, Sargint?' sez I.

"'This way, ye blundherin' man, an' don't you be doin'
ut,' sez he. Wid that he shows me a Waster action—the
breech av her all cut away to show the inside—an' so plazed
was he to grumble that he dimonstrated fwhat Hogan had

done twice over. 'An' that comes av not knowin' the wep-
ping you're purvided wid,' sez he.

" 'Thank ye, Sargint,' sez I ; I will come to you again for
further information.'

" 'Ye will not,' sez he. 'Kape your clanin'-rod away
from the breech-pin or you will get into throuble.'

" I wint outside an' I could ha' danced wid delight for the
grandeur av ut. 'They will load my rifle, good luck to thim,
whoile I'm away,' thinks I, and back I wint to the Canteen
to give them their clear chanst.

" The Canteen was fillin' wid men at the ind av the day.
I made feign to be far gone in dhrink, an', wan by wan, all
my roomful came in wid Vulmea. I wint away, walkin'
thick and heavy, but not so thick an' heavy that àny wan
cud ha' tuk me. Sure and thrue, there was a kyartridge
gone from my pouch an' lyin' snug in my rifle. I was hot
wid rage against thim all, and I worried the bullet out wid
my teeth as fast as I cud, the room bein' empty. Then I
tuk my boot un' the clanin'-road and knocked out the pin
av the fallin'-block. O 'twas music when that pin rowled
on the flure ! I put ut into my pouch an' stuck a dab av dirt
on the holes in the plate, puttin' the fallin'-block back.
' That'll do your buisness, Vulmea,' sez I, lyin' easy on the
cot. 'Come an' sit on my chest the whole room av you, an'
I will take you to my bosom for the biggest divils that iver
cheated halter.' I wud have no mercy on Vulmea. His oi
or his life—little I cared !

" At dusk they came back, the twelve av thim, an' they
had all been dhrinkin'. I was shammin' sleep on the cot.
Wan man wint outside in the verandah. Whin he whishtled
they began to rage roun' the room an' carry on tremenjus.
But I niver want to hear men laugh as they did—skylarkin'
too ! 'Twas like mad jackals.

" 'Shtop that blasted noise !' sez O'Hara in the dark, an'
pop goes the room lamp. I cud hear O'Hara runnin' up an'
the rattlin' av my rifle in the rack an' the men breathin'

heavy as they stud roun' my cot. I cud see O'Hara in the
light av the verandah lamp, an' thin I heard the crack av my
rifle. She cried loud, poor darlint, bein' mishandled. Next
minut' five men were houldin' me down. 'Go easy,' I sez ;
'fwhat's ut all about ?'

"Thin Vulmea, on the flure, raised a howl you cud hear
from wan ind av cantonmints to the other. 'I'm dead, I'm
butchered, I'm blind!' sez he. 'Saints have mercy on my
sinful sowl! Sind for Father Constant! C sind for Father
Constant an' let me go clean!' By that I knew he was not
so dead as I cud ha' wished.

"O'Hara picks up the lamp in the verandah wid a hand
as stiddy as a rest. 'Fwhat damned dog's thrick is this av
yours ?' sez he, and turns the light on Tim Vulmea that was
shwimmin' in blood from top to toe. The fallin'-block had
sprung free behin' a full charge av powther—good care I tuk
to bite down the brass afther takin' out the bullet that there
might be somethin' to give ut full worth—an' had. cut Tim
from the lip to the corner av the right eye, lavin' the eyelid
in tatthers, an' so up an' along by the forehead to the hair.
'Twas more av a rakin' plough, if you will ondherstand, than
a clean cut ; an' niver did I see a man bleed as Vulmea did.
The dhrink an' the stew that he was in pumped the blood
strong. The minut' the men sittin' on my chest heard
O'Hara spakin' they scatthered each wan to his cot, an' cried
out very politeful : 'Fwhat is ut, Sargint ?'

"'Fwhat is ut!' sez O'Hara, shakin' Tim. 'Well an' good
do you know fwhat ut is, ye skulkin' ditch-lurkin' dogs! Get
a *doolie*, an' take this whimperin' scutt away. There will be
more heard av ut than any av you will care for.'

"Vulmea sat up rockin' his head in his hand an' moanin'
for Father Constant.

"'Be done!' sez O'Hara, dhraggin' him up by the hair.
'You're none so dead that you cannot go fifteen years for
thryin' to shoot me.'

"'I did not.' sez Vulmea · 'I was shootin' mesilf'

" ' That's quare,' sez O'Hara, ' for the front av my jackut is black wid your powther.' He tuk up the rifle that was still warm an' began to laugh. ' I'll make your life Hell to you,' sez he, ' for attempted murdher an' kapin' your rifle onproperly. You'll be hanged first an' thin put undher stoppages for four fifteen. The rifle's done for,' sez he.

" ' Why, 'tis my rifle ! ' sez I, comin' up to look ; ' Vulmea ye divil, fwhat were you doin' wid her—answer me that ? '

" ' Lave me alone,' sez Vulmea ; ' I'm dyin' ! '

" ' I'll wait till you're betther,' sez I, ' an' thin we two will talk ut out umbrageous.'

" O'Hara pitched Tim nto the *doolie,* none too tinder, but all the bhoys kep' by their cots, which was not the sign av' innocint men. I was huntin' ivrywhere for my fallin'-block, but not findin' ut at all. I niver found ut.

" ' *Now* fwhat will I do ? ' sez O'Hara, swingin' the verandah light in his hand an' lookin' down the room. I had hate an' contimpt av O'Hara an' I have now, dead tho' he is, but, for all that, will I say he was a brave man. He is baskin' in Purgathory this tide, but I wish he cud hear that, whin he stud lookin' down the room an' the bhoys shivered before the oi av him, I knew him for a brave man an' I liked him *so.*

" ' Fwhat will I do ? ' sez O'Hara agin, an' we heard the voice av a woman low an' sof' in the verandah. 'Twas Slimmy's wife, come over at the shot, sittin' on wan av the benches an' scarce able to walk.

" ' Oh Denny—Denny dear,' sez she, ' have they kilt you ? '

" O'Hara looked down the room again an' showed his teeth to the gum. Then he spat on the flure.

" ' You're not worth ut,' sez he. ' Light that lamp, ye dogs,' an' wid that he turned away, an' I saw him walkin' off wid Slimmy's wife ; she thryin' to wipe off the powther-black on the front av his jackut wid her handkerchief. ' A brave man you are,' thinks I—' a brave man an' a bad woman.'

" No wan said a word for a time. They was all ashamed past spache.

" ' Fwhat d'you think he will do ? ' sez wan av thim at last. ' He knows we're all in ut.'

" ' Are we so ? ' sez I from my cot. ' The man that sez that to me will be hurt. I do not know,' sez I, ' fwhat onderhand divilmint you have conthrived, but by what I've seen I know that you cannot commit murdher wid another man's rifle— such shakin' cowards you are. I'm goin' to slape,' I sez, ' an' you can blow my head off whoile I lay.' I did not slape, though, for a long time. Can ye wonder ?

" Next morn the news was through all the rig'mint, an' there was nothin' that the men did not tell. O'Hara reports, fair an' easy, that Vulmea was come to grief through tamperin, wid his rifle in barricks, all for to show the mechanism. An' by my sowl, he had the impart'nince to say that he was on the shpot at the time an' cud certify that ut was an accidint ! You might ha' knocked my roomful down wid a straw whin they heard that. 'Twas lucky for thim that the bhoys were always thryin' to find out how the new rifle was made, an' a lot av thim had come up for easin' the pull by shtickin' bits av grass an' such in the part av the lock that showed near the thrigger. The first issues of the 'Tinis was not covered in, an' I mesilf have eased the pull av mine time an' agin. A light pull is ten points on the range to me.

" ' I will not have this foolishness ! ' sez the Colonel. ' I will twist the tail off Vulmea ! ' sez he ; but whin he saw him, all tied up an' groanin' in hospital, he changed his will. ' Make him an early convalescint,' sez he to the Doctor, an' Vulmea was made so for a warnin'. His big bloody bandages an' face puckered up to wan side did more to kape the bhoys from messin' wid the insides av their rifles than any punishmint.

" O'Hara gave no reason for fwhat he'd said, an' all my roomful were too glad to enquire, tho' he put his spite upon thim more wearin' than before. Wan day, howiver, he tuk me apart very polite, for he cud be that at the choosin'.

" ' You're a good sodger, tho' you're a damned insolint man,' sez he.

"'Fair words, Sargint,' sez I, 'or I may be insolent again.'

"''Tis not like you,' sez he, 'to lave your rifle in the rack widout the breech-pin, for widout the breech-pin she was whin Vulmea fired. I should ha' found the break av ut in the eyes av the holes, else,' he sez.

"'Sargint,' sez I, 'fwhat wud your life ha' been worth av the breech-pin had been in place, for, on my sowl, my life wud be worth just as much to me av I tould you whether ut was or was not. Be thankful the bullet was not there,' I sez.

"'That's thrue,' sez he, pulling his moustache; 'but I do not believe that you, for all your lip, was in that business.'

"'Sargint,' sez I, 'I cud hammer the life out av a man in ten minuts wid my fistes if that man dishpleased me; for I am a good sodger, an' I will be threated as such, an' whoile my fistes are my own they're strong enough for all work I have to do. They do not fly back towards me!' sez I, lookin' him betune the eyes.

"'You're a good man,' sez he, lookin' me betune the eyes —an' O he was a gran'-built man to see—'You're a good man,' he sez, 'an' I cud wish, for the pure frolic av ut, that I was not a Sargint, or that you were not a Privit; an' you will think me no coward whin I say this thing.'

"'I do not,' sez I. 'I saw you whin Vulmea mishandled the rifle. But Sargint,' I sez, 'take the wurrd from me now, spakin' as man to man wid the shtripes off, tho' 'tis little right I have to talk, me being fwhat I am by natur'. This time ye tuk no harm, an' next time ye may not, but, in the ind, so sure as Slimmy's wife came into the verandah, so sure will ye take harm—an' bad harm. Have thought, Sargint,' sez I. 'Is ut worth ut?'

"'Yer're a bould man,' sez he, breathin' harrd. 'A very bould man. But I am a bould man tu. Do you go your way, Privit Mulvaney, an' I will go mine.'

"We had no further spache thin or afther, but, wan by another he drafted the twelve av my room out into other rooms an' got thim spread among the Comp'nies, for they was not a good breed to live together, an' the Comp'ny orf'cers saw ut. They wud ha' shot me in the night av they had known fwhat I knew; but that they did not.

"An', in the ind, as I said, O'Hara met his death from Rafferty for foolin' wid his wife. He wint his own way too well—Eyah, too well! Shtraight to that affair, widout turnin' to the right or to the lef', he wint, an' may the Lord have mercy on his sowl. Amin!"

"'Ear! 'Ear!" said Ortheris, pointing the moral with a wave of his pipe. "An' this is 'im 'oo would be a bloomin' Vulmea all for the sake of Mullins an' a bloomin' button! Mullins never went after a woman in his life. Mrs. Mullins, she saw 'im one day——"

"Ortheris," I said, hastily, for the romances of Private Ortheris are slightly too daring for publication, "look at the sun. It's a quarter past six!"

"O Lord! Three quarters of an hour for five an' a' arf miles! We'll 'ave to run like Jimmy O."

The Three Musketeers clambered on to the bridge and departed hastily in the direction of the cantonment road. When I overtook them I offered them two stirrups and a tail, which they accepted enthusiastically. Ortheris held the tail, and in this manner we trotted steadily through the shadows by an unfrequented road.

At the turn into the cantonments we heard carriage wheels. It was the Colonel's barouche, and in it sat the Colonel's wife and daughter. I caught a suppressed chuckle, and my beast sprang forward with a lighter step.

The Three Musketeers had vanished into the night.

L'ENVOI.

And they were stronger hands than mine
   That digged the Ruby from the earth—
   More cunning brains that made it worth
The large desire of a King ;
And bolder hearts that through the brine
   Went down the Perfect Pearl to bring.

Lo, I have wrought in common clay
   Rude figures of a rough-hewn race ;
   For Pearls strew not the market-place
In this my town of banishment,
Where with the shifting dust I play
   And eat the bread of Discontent.

Yet is there life in that I make,—
   O Thou who knowest, turn and see,
   As Thou hast power over me,
So have I power over these,
Because I wrought them for Thy sake,
   And breathed in them mine agonies.

Small mirth was in the making.   Now
   I lift the cloth that clokes the clay,
   And, wearied, at Thy feet I lay
My wares ere I go forth to sell.
The long *bazar* will praise—but Thou—
   Heart of my heart, have I done well ?

OPINIONS OF THE PRESS.

The *Home and Colonial Mail* says :—The foibles of Anglo-Indian society have been frequently sketched, and some full-blossomed incident of Indian life has budded into the three-volume novel before to-day ; but we doubt if anything has ever been written about society in India which can compare in brilliancy and originality to the sketches of Mr. Rudyard Kipling, a new writer, who is assuredly destined to make a distinct mark in literature. Mr. Kipling, who would doubtless come under Mr. Robert Buchanan's ban as a pessimistic young man, has a power of observation truly marvellous, and as this faculty is combined with another equally rare—that of recording what he observes with caustic and brilliant touches—the result is easy to imagine. It is true that Mr. Kipling lays himself open to the remark that he is a cynic as well as a humorist, but Thackeray came in for little compliments of this kind, and Mr. Kipling will, no doubt, endeavour to bear himself with becoming modesty under such circumstances.

His knowledge of Anglo-Indian human nature, which is ordinary human nature under great provocation, is profound—we were going to say awful—and he can go from grave to gay with the facility of a true artist. His dialogue is extremely clever, and we venture to think that he is not likely to confine his attention to the miniature world he has depicted so well, but will take a wider field. Should he turn his attention to writing for the stage he ought to score a great success. In *The Story of the Gadsbys* and *Under the Deodars,* Mr. Kipling deals with society at Simla. *Soldiers Three* is dedicated to Tommy Atkins, and is an instance of its author's versatility. In *Black and White* he deals with native life, and here, too, Mr. Kipling is quite at home. All these books are written in a style all the author's own, and they only require to be known on this side to be appreciated. They are published by Messrs. Wheeler & Co. of Allahabad, who have shown considerable enterprise in issuing these volumes in cheap form. Well got up, with covers artistically designed, each conveying a characteristic idea, these little volumes would do credit to any library.

The *Civil and Military Gazette* says :—The stories show the versatility of the writer. In *Soldiers Three* he is completely the master of three separate dialects (shall we call them ?), and of the soldier's vocabulary and mode of thought and expression. In the *Story of the Gadsbys* we have charmingly and characteristically sketched the character of a bright young girl developed, later on, into the loving and tender wife. His pictures of Anglo-Indian life are finished works of art, full of go and brightness, true to nature in its many aspects, and enlivened with a quaint fancy, a ready wit, and a faculty of phrase and expression seldom met with.

NEW COPYRIGHT WORKS

SPECIALLY WRITTEN FOR

A. H. WHEELER & CO.'S INDIAN RAILWAY LIBRARY.

1. **"Soldiers Three:"** Stories of Barrack-Room Life. By Rudyard Kipling
2. **"The Story of the Gadsbys:"** A Tale without a Plot. By   „
3. **"In Black and White:"** Stories of Native Life. By   „
4. **"Under the Deodars:"** In Social Byeways. By   „

(The above four numbers are illustrative of the four main features of Anglo-Indian life, viz., The Military, Domestic, Native and Social.)

5. **"The Phantom Rickshaw,"** and other Eerie Tales. By Rudyard Kipling.
6. **"Wee Willie Winkie,"** and other Child Stories. By   „
7. **"The Colonel's Crime:"** A Romance of To-day. By Ivan O'Beirne.

IN THE PRESS AND TO BE ISSUED SHORTLY.

"**The Subaltern, the Policeman and the Little Girl.**"
"**Under the Rose.**" By Ivan O'Beirne.
"**The One-eyed Forger,**" and other Detective Stories. By R. Reid.

Other volumes to follow.

In specially designed **Picture Covers.   Price one Rupee.**

The first 7 numbers published are now procurable at all Railway Bookstalls or from A. H. WHEELER & Co., Allahabad

BY RUDYARD KIPLING.

PLAIN TALES FROM THE HILLS, Cloth   ... Rs. 4 0 0
DEPARTMENTAL DITTIES, Cloth ...   ... „ 2 8 0

At all Railway Bookstalls or from A. H. Wheeler & Co., Allahabad

FOR OPINIONS OF THE PRESS, SEE OVERLEAF.

PUBLICATIONS OF
THE R. S. SURTEES SOCIETY

R. S. SURTEES

Mr. Sponge's Sporting Tour. Facsimile of 1853 edition. 13 full-page coloured plates and 90 engravings by **John Leech.** Introduction by **Auberon Waugh.**

Mr. Facey Romford's Hounds. 24 coloured plates by **Leech** and **'Phiz'.** 50 engravings by **W. T. Maud.** Introduction by **Enoch Powell.**

"Ask Mamma". Facsimile of 1858 edition, 13 coloured plates and 70 engravings by **Leech.** Introduction by **Rebecca West.**

Handley Cross; or **Mr. Jorrocks' Hunt.** Facsimile of 1854 edition. 17 coloured plates and 100 engravings by **Leech.** Introduction by **Raymond Carr.**

Jorrocks' Jaunts and Jollities. Facsimile of 1874 edition. 31 coloured plates by **Henry Alken, 'Phiz'** and **W. Heath.** Introduction by **Michael Wharton** ('Peter Simple').

Hillingdon Hall or **The Cockney Squire** (Mr. Jorrocks). Facsimile of 1888 edition. 12 coloured plates by **Wildrake, W. Heath** and **Jellicoe.** Introduction by **Robert Blake.**

Plain or Ringlets? Facsimile of 1860 edition. 13 coloured plates and 45 engravings by **Leech.** Introduction by **Molly Keane.**

Price **£14.95** in each case, packing and postage included.

Separate sets of coloured plates **£5** each (including p. & p.)

The Horseman's Manual: being a treatise on Soundness, of the Law of Warranty and generally on the Laws relating to Horses. Surtees's first book, published in 1831. Hugh Davidson has published a numbered facsimile edition of 600 copies, of which 38 remain.
Price **£10.50,** packing and postage included.

John Leech
and the Victorian Scene

Simon Houfe's magnificent book on Leech (published by the Antique Collectors' Club) is offered to all subscribers for books of the R. S. Surtees Society, whether under this or previous offers, at the price of **£19.50** (including p. & p.), compared with the normal retail price of £22.50.

It contains 130 illustrations, many in colour.

SOME EXPERIENCES *AND* FURTHER EXPERIENCES OF AN IRISH R.M. *AND* IN MR. KNOX'S COUNTRY

by E. OE. Somerville and Martin Ross.

Some Experiences, Further Experiences and *In Mr. Knox's Country* contain thirty-five episodes in which Major Sinclair Yeates recounts, with sober dignity, humour and tolerance, his social and professional discomfitures as a Resident Magistrate in South-West Ireland at the turn of the century. The rhetoric and deceit of the natives provide the wit and drama. Circumstances make Major Yeates a connoisseur of whole-hearted insincerity.

The R. S. Surtees Society's editions of *Some Experiences, Further Experiences* and *In Mr. Knox's Country* are as nearly as practicable facsimiles of the first editions, of 1899, 1908 and 1915 respectively. They include the black and white illutrations by **Miss Somerville** from the first editions (30 in *Some Experiences,* 35 in *Further Experiences* and 8 in *Mr. Knox*). Introduction by **Molly Keane.**

Price **£7.95** in each case, packing and postage included.

IRISH R.M. SET OF THREE

The price of a set of *In Mr. Knox's Country, Some Experiences* and *Further Experiences of an Irish R.M.* is **£21.00,** including packing and postage.

CAPTAIN GRONOW'S REMINISCENCES AND RECOLLECTIONS *AND* LAST RECOLLECTIONS

Gronow served in the Peninsula War, fought at Quartre Bras and Waterloo and was with the allied armies in Paris when the Bourbons were restored. Thereafter, in London and Paris, he lived the life of a dandy "committing the greatest follies without in the slightest disturbing the points of his shirt collar." As a ranconteur he is superb, with vivid accounts of Waterloo, the coup d'etat of 1851, of balls and battles, of duellists, gamblers, dukes and opera singers.

The Society's editions are facsimiles of the Joseph Grego editions of 1889 and include all his 25 coloured plates from original and contemporary sources – "and a very handsome set they make" – Paul Johnson in The Spectator.

Prices **£14.95** for *Reminiscences and Recollections,* **£13.95** for *Last Recollections.*

GOOD INTENTIONS in WAPPING

SHIP'S COMPANY   by W. W. JACOBS

What was Wapping like before Rupert Murdoch, before the G.L.C., before the Port of London Authority, before the Germans bombed it flat, indeed before the First War and before the Trades Disputes Act, 1906 had had much effect—in fact only a decade after the Diamond Jubilee?

W. W. Jacobs (1863–1943) was born and brought up in Wapping where his father was a wharfinger. According to Michael Sadleir, in the D.N.B., he recalled his childhood days, when "with his brothers and sisters he ran wild in Wapping, as happy interludes in a life of nagging discomfort."

Like Conrad, Kipling and E. Nesbit he was a contributor to the Strand Magazine in its great days. Like Surtees, Jacobs was well served by his illustrators. He was popular with high, middle and low brows from about 1895 to 1930, by which latter date P. G. Wodehouse had overtaken him.

Jacobs' best short stories were about Wapping and the best of these were told by the night-watchman who, sitting on his wharf, recounted the adventures of his friends Sam Small, Peter Russet, Ginger Dick and others.

W. W. Jacobs' SHIP'S COMPANY is a set of 12 short stories, first published in 1908. The title is uninformative and perhaps a little misleading since the action all takes place on land—near, but not on, salt water. Some of the characters, it is true, arrive and depart by sea.

The best of all the stories in SHIP'S COMPANY is *Good Intentions,* in which the night-watchman is both the hero and the narrator. The plot is complicated, but entirely clear and credible—in fact, better and faster than the plots of most French farces. *Good Intentions in Wapping* might have been a better title for the set than SHIP'S COMPANY.

The R. S. Surtees Society's edition is a facsimile of the first (1908) edition and includes the 23 black and white illustrations by **Will Owen** in the first edition. Will Owen (1869–1957) was a Punch artist, a close friend of W. W. Jacobs and, like Leech, 'Phiz' and Edith Somerville, was completely familiar with the subjects he was drawing. It was he who drew the famous Bisto Kids advertisement.